Rixen

HOLIDATE WITH AN ALIEN

ELLA BLAKE

I'm visiting my daughter and her Stryxian mate for the holidays, but a certain gorgeous merchant has thoroughly captured my attention. I thought I was well past these fluttery feelings, but Rixen ties my tongue in knots and makes my heart pound. He keeps to himself, but when we team up to prepare the settlement for the upcoming festival, I know the sparks fly in both directions. But how do I get a grumpy alien to admit his feelings for me?

———

Rubi is lovely in every way, but the feisty human female isn't planning to stay on Stryxia. Her home is on Earth. I've no interest in a brief romance. I want Rubi as my mate, permanently, but that isn't on her agenda. Still, I agree to work with her on the upcoming human-Stryxian festivities. When one of my transports, which is carrying supplies to my settlement, is disabled out on the Sanrous Plains, I head out to repair it. In a moment of weakness, I agree to let Rubi come along for the ride. It shouldn't take more than a day, after all. But the problems with the transport ship are a little more complicated than they appear. It seems Rubi and I are in for a bumpy—and very surprising—ride.

———

Holidate with an Alien is a collaboration of some of Science Fiction Romance's best authors! Our holiday present to our readers: fun, steamy, romantic adventures that revolve around one or more holidates! Read them all, in any order. Honey Phillips, Ava Ross, Ella Maven, Ella Blake, Tana Stone, Rena Marks, and Alana Khan. Curl up with a cup of hot cocoa and enjoy!

CHAPTER

One

Rubi

I'D BEEN on Stryxia one other time before. That time, the domes had still arched over the Trakia settlement, shielding it from the not-yet-optimal conditions on the surface. The planet had been wrecked by the Morr-ta, a warring species that had targeted Earth, too. Thanks to the Stryxians' help, the Morr-ta hadn't ravaged our planet. Stryxia had not fared well, however. Their natural resources had been stripped. Habitats destroyed. It had taken years of diligent work and a technology that Earth could only imagine, to restore Stryxia to its natural state.

I walked down the main pathway of the Trakia settlement—more like a town, now—and saw the clear, lavender sky above. No more domes. Water flowed through riverbanks. Plants flourished. The creatures that had roamed this land were breeding and living again (thanks to a genome bank that had preserved most species' genetic material). I didn't know what it was like before the Morr-ta ravaged the land, but it was beautiful, now. The air was clear and warm.

Stryxia flourished again. And there was another welcome addition, which hadn't been present during my last visit—the sound of children. Babies, specifically. More women had come to Stryxia, where the birthrate of females had fallen below sustainable levels. *Women* had been the price they'd requested for help in defeating the Morr-ta and driving them away from Earth. It had been in the form of a lottery for single women of childbearing age. Now, it was voluntary.

My daughter, Andromeda, hadn't come here voluntarily, but she *had* found her true love among the ridiculously attractive males of Stryxia. Her mate, Xarik, was an absolute dish, and now that they were expecting their first child together, I wondered how often I could come out here with the new visa system that Earth and Stryxia had set up. Stryxia didn't want humans overrunning their fragile planet with their cameras and trash. Only residents could come and go as they pleased, and to become a resident, you had to be mated to a Stryxian.

That wasn't likely to happen in my case. At fifty-six, I was too old to make babies, and the one older male to whom I felt an attraction, made it clear he wasn't in the market for a mate. Period.

I'd leave him alone if I didn't have business. As the only merchant in Trakia who traded with Earth, I had a list of items for him to procure from my home world. I'd brought as much as I could, but there had been no way to carry all the holiday paraphernalia on the passenger transport that brought me here. Plus, I hadn't realized I'd be staying longer. Andromeda and Xarik had surprised me with news of the baby and I wanted to be here to meet the baby, who was due shortly before Christmas. There were too many planets to keep track of these days.

The trees were different here, obviously. Still tall and majestic, but they branched differently, and the foliage came in a wide variety of colors, unlike our typical green on Earth. The streets were exceptionally unique. Made of a special enhanced stone called *corsic*. It changed temperature, so the stones cooled on hot days, and warmed on cold days, helping to regulate the overall air temperature. I'd never heard of such a clever thing until visiting this planet. The Stryxians were far more advanced than us in many ways. When visiting here, everyone had to sign documents promising we wouldn't introduce the tech we were exposed to, to Earth. It annoyed every tech company on my home planet that Stryxia doled out technology in tiny increments. Many humans found it condescending, but having spent time here, I understood. We had some catching up to do in order to manage the tech we had, let alone anything new.

The row of shops was like something out of medieval Europe, but with technology. Prices and goods were projected, glowing in midair, as a monitoring bot scanned anyone who approached the shop and either assisted, or summoned the Stryxian shopkeeper. I spent a lot of time browsing the available merchandise, marveling at the differences between our species, and, yes, haggling. That, apparently, was an activity that transcended species and solar systems.

Rixen's shop had no signs, bots, or projected prices. It looked as ordinary as any other building. Upon entering, the first thing you saw was a plain, black counter. Nothing else. I'd been in here before. A few days ago, I'd ordered a bunch of baby items. Today, I came armed with another list. Rixen, I feared, would not be pleased with it.

I stepped up to the simple black counter. When I touched it, the surface changed from black to blue and illuminated from the inside. It put off quite a light, probably so the keeper of the shop knew a customer had arrived. A gruff voice called out from a room in the back, "Coming in a moment."

It was taking me a while to get used to the translator device. It hugged the back of my ear and only put a slight delay on the Stryxian words translated to my language. The more familiar I became with it, the faster it was. My brain was adapting. It was nice to see the gray material in my old head could still pick up new tricks now and then.

I tried not to react when the tall, gorgeous shape of Rixen appeared in the doorway and walked up to the counter. My body had the same reaction every time I saw him. First, shock. Then, the mad scramble to regain my composure, and finally, an insidious warmth that stole through every limb. I swear, half my brain shut down whenever I was around this male, and I considered myself pretty sharp. But not when Rixen was around. It was embarrassing how simple my thoughts became in his presence.

He sighed at the sight of me. "Rubi. How can I help you?" He did *not* sound as if he wanted to help me. He sounded as if he wanted me to leave. Immediately.

"Hello, Rixen."

"Most people call me Rix," he said, referring to the fact that I always called him by his full name.

"I'm not most people." I hadn't intended that to be flirty, but it definitely came out that way.

The smallest smile twitched his lips. "That is undoubtedly true."

I put on my most winning smile, deciding not to try to interpret his cryptic expression. "I have a few things I would like ordered from Earth," I said, pulling the list from my bag.

"I told you, I'm not permitted to import the type of gin you—"

I waved my hand, cutting him off. "I'm not trying to buy alcohol," I said. I had, though. I should have brought my own bottle of gin.

"Then what is it that you want this time?"

The thing about Rixen was, I was pretty sure we had had a connection when we first set eyes on each other. It had been like a mini lightning bolt struck me. It was my first time to Stryxia. I had just met my daughter's charming mate, Xarik. He was showing me around the settlement. My gaze met Rixen's, and it felt as if time stopped for a moment.

It was ridiculous. It was the kind of thing that happened to teenagers, not cynical widows like myself. After losing my husband to the war, I never expected to feel anything like that again, so the connection felt significant. Like it meant something. And I wasn't foolish enough to not know the difference between a friendly look and an *I-find-you-attractive* look.

Rixen found me attractive, initially. He just didn't any longer. It was a shame, but I had been through enough loss, enough struggle, to not allow something like an unrequited crush to be anything more than a disappointment.

But I *still* needed his help to get the things I wanted for Andi's first holidays on Stryxia. She loved her new homeland, but that didn't mean she had to give up all the things she loved on Earth, too. Especially since I was here. While she was focusing on her baby, I could make arrangements to give her a taste of her old home. And I suspected the other women here would enjoy that as well.

I handed Rix the list I had prepared and steeled myself for his reply. He was the only merchant currently licensed to get goods to and from Earth. There was a lot of regulation here. Stryxia was particular about what came from Earth and what went to it, and I knew that what I was asking for was odd.

Rix raised his dark, brooding eyebrows. He was tall

and broad, with a barrel chest and large hands. His dark gray scales were shiny and purple-tinged. Scales deepened in color with age, either bluish or purple. His face was just about the most handsome one I'd ever seen. He had a strong nose and gorgeous lips. Grooves ran on either side of his mouth, highlighting a strong jaw. God, he was easy to look at. He had a voice to weaken the knees, too. It was low with a touch of gravel. Ugh. Such a shame he wasn't interested. His black eyes gazed at me over the list. "I cannot do this."

"Why not?" I asked. "Nothing on this list is banned."

"That is not true. Evergreen trees are not native to Stryxia. Bringing one here would require multiple approvals before we could even put in the request to Earth."

"Okay." I lifted my chin, undeterred. "Tell me what I have to fill out. Pine trees are a custom of my people this time of year to celebrate the Christmas holiday."

"And this is an awful lot of candles." He shook his head. "Paraffin wax is—"

"Then let's go with beeswax, or bayberry, or anything that's approved. We like candles for the holidays," I said.

"Why?" He sounded bewildered. "Our homes have excellent illumination."

"Candles are homey and warm," I explained. "And some are scented. But there's something about an open flame that just says 'holidays.' You know?"

"No. I do *not* know. Open flames are pointlessly

hazardous, but not banned." He shook his head and inputted my order and looked at the next thing on the list. "What are these, *noisemakers*, and why would you want such things?"

"Those would be for New Years Eve." I knew he had to inquire about the items we ordered from Earth to know if they were a restricted item or not, but did he have to do so with such a frown? I gave him a wink to try and get him to loosen up. "We bring in the new year with cheering, kisses, and noisemakers. Don't worry, they're not *that* loud."

He glanced up. "Exactly how many holidays do your people celebrate this time of year?"

I raised one brow. "So many, all over the world, I don't even know them all. I can recite the ones I know if—"

He held up a hand. "Forget it. I do not need to know all of your holidays. You have way too many. That is all I need to know." He looked back at the list. "String lights. These are too many."

Good god. Did he have to be a grump about everything? "We hang them around our homes and neighborhoods," I said in a clipped voice. "It's festive."

"But other human females have ordered them, too. The result will be enough to string through half the settlement," he said. "Is that what you intend to do?"

I cocked a hip and met his gaze. "Maybe?"

He shook his head. "You need permission to do something like that."

"My son-in-law and daughter are commanders of this base, aren't they?"

One corner of his very sexy mouth curled upwards. "Yes, but *you* are not. And neither of them has authorized any of this."

"Fine. I'll talk to Xarik. He would be happy to give his mate and the other women living in this place, a taste of their home traditions."

"I am all for traditions," Rix said. "Even human ones." There was a bite to his voice as he said the word *human*, and for the first time I wondered if he had a problem with my kind. I'd never gotten that impression before. He didn't sound too pleased, though, when saying the name of my species.

I frowned. "Does it bother you that we're here?"

Rixen did not look up from his screen. "I am glad you are here. Our species would die out without your breeding females."

"Wow, what an endorsement."

He sighed and rubbed his eyes. "Human females are breathing life back into Stryxia in many ways." He met my gaze. "The ones that stay, that is."

Oh, *now* I understood. I was a tourist. An interloper. Not a Stryxian resident. And I could not contribute to the gene pool at all, thanks to being past reproductive age. The insinuation that I was unworthy of being here because I couldn't *breed*, flared every furious nerve in my body. How dare he? How had I ever thought he was attractive?

I narrowed my eyes and jabbed a finger in his direction. "You can get every single thing on that list. I know you can. And I have the credits, so I expect to get them." I could have left it at that. I *should* have. "And I'll just add that if you truly valued the women who have come here, forsaking their home planet and embracing an entirely new society to *breed* with you, you'd get as many goddamn string lights as the transport can hold." I slapped my hand on the counter, really pissed off now. "Even when the female ordering them is as useless as I am."

His brow snapped into a confused, uneven frown. "Useless? What madness are you speaking, female?"

"You know exactly what I mean," I said. "I'm useless here. I understand. I get it."

His eyes flared wide. "No. That is not at all what I am—"

But I was beyond listening at this point. Blood was pumping hard in my veins. My stupid ego was tweaked terribly, and I knew my face was as red as a beet. "Oh no, you were very clear," I said, cutting him off before he could say another word, and probably make it worse. "I'll have you know, family connections are very close on Earth. My daughter and I are very close." I narrowed my eyes as a new thought occurred to me. "Or maybe you have an issue with the father of my grandchild being Vanyi?"

Xarik was a unique member of his people. He had pale silver scales and possessed the unique ability to read others' minds and control them, if he wished. Vanyi powers had, at one point, made Stryxians of his kind feared and loathed. In fact, it had been a Vanyi Stryxian who had attempted to take over the planet and had been responsible for my darling Andromeda's abduction from Earth. That Vanyi, Sleer, had been killed by Xarik to save my daughter's life. His act had told me really all I needed to know about my son-in-law. He would do anything to protect her. But negative sentiment about Vanyi remained. Plenty of Stryxians still looked at them with suspicion, uncomfortable with the power they held. Once revered sages and wise ones, they had become feared. That was changing now, but older Stryxians, like Rixen, could still harbor prejudice.

"No." It was Rixen's turn to be angry. His chest expanded and his eyes darkened. "Xarik is, and has always been, a close friend. I welcome the arrival of his offspring."

I gave him a brittle smile. "Good. Then you will see that the items I have requested arrive without issue." I couldn't keep the hard-ass act up, or the anger. I just didn't have it in me. "I want my future grandchild to have a lovely first Christmas. You should see a newborn baby when they look at the tree, all decorated. They can't see well, so they just gaze at the lights in pure wonder."

I knew I had won. Rix shook his head, shoulders slumping. "I will see what I can do, Rubi. But I cannot guarantee the tree. What is the genus and species of the tree?"

"What? A spruce or a fir, I think."

"You don't know?"

"I'm not a tree expert," I said, getting annoyed again. "Maybe it's a balsam."

His hand paused over his screen. "If I'm going to put in the request for a live, non-native tree to be delivered to Stryxia, I need the exact species name to input for analysis of possible environmental contamination."

I held up a hand. "I don't know the exact species of a Christmas tree. There are a bunch used and they don't have species information on them when you buy one. If you can't get a live Earth tree, get an artificial one."

His face screwed up in confusion. "They make ones that aren't real?"

"Yes. Some people like them. They store them in their attics the rest of the year, but I prefer real ones for the smell."

He wrinkled his nose. "They smell?"

"Yes, like a pine tree." I realized I had no idea how to describe that to someone on an alien planet. "It's a *good* smell. Woodsy, sharp, pleasant."

He shook his head. "Your people are strange."

I put my hands on my hips. "So are yours."

And with that magnificent rebuttal, I turned and left his shop. It annoyed me now that I was going to give him credits for being kind of an ass. It stung more than I would've liked, to hear what he thought of women who couldn't bear children to Stryxian males. If only I were younger…

No. Fuck that. I shook that thought off. I *had* my children. In fact, one of my children was here, soon to have a baby with a Stryxian male. If that didn't earn me the right to be here, I didn't know what did. And it wasn't as if I was staying. I squared my shoulders and headed back to my cottage. I was here to visit Andromeda and Xarik. I planned to support them in the early days of parenthood as they needed. I was *not* here to win the approval of a pompous, asinine Stryxian merchant named Rixen.

CHAPTER
Two

Rixen

I WAS NOT sure what just happened. I had deeply insulted Rubi in some manner, but I wasn't sure how. What I had said to make her furious was a mystery to me. She implied that I only valued females who could breed, which was absurd.

After all, I was older than Rubi. I knew I would never be chosen by a young female as a mate, and I would not want to be. There were young virile males far better suited to take a mate and start a family. I had lost that window in the Morr-ta war, when the birth rates of my people had critically declined.

There had simply been no females for my *mala* to identify a mate to bond with. The few offspring produced were mostly male. The whole initial reason we had agreed to assist the humans was to establish a lottery system to bring human females into our breeding pool to try to save our species. It had been fairly mercenary, but it evolved into something else entirely. Our males' *malas*—our soul centers—had awoken, identifying true bonds with the humans. The result was Stryxian males who deeply loved their human mates. The bondings were as real as if both mates were Stryxian. The offspring these matings produced were strong, and importantly, of both genders. Males *and* females were being born, possessing the best traits of both of our species. The offspring looked different than both humans and Stryxians, but were adored and loved by both.

I entered Rubi's order into my system, wondering what, exactly, I had said that had upset her so much. The fire in her eyes had flared hot. Her skin had flushed and I imagined a different scenario that would bring out her fire other than temper. She would be a magnificent bed partner.

Unfortunately, her little display made her even more appealing to me. That was not something I needed. She was appealing enough as it was. I had been entranced by that female the moment I laid eyes on her. She was stunning. Beautiful, deep red hair, with some gray, like me. At first glance you might think her eyes were black, but no. They were the deepest blue.

Her daughter, and now Xarik, shared the color, except they both had gold rings around them. But not Rubi. Her eyes were the color of deep water—mysterious and unknowing. I had been transfixed the moment I saw her, from across the town square on her first visit here.

I had felt a yearning so acute, I could feel and see nothing else, only her. My eyes had burned. Eye irritation *was* the early sign that a *mala* had identified a mate. But it could also have been an allergy to something I'd brought into the shop. I'd hoped it was the latter, because while the burning in my eyes had filled me with hope and a sensation of completion, I'd learned that she was only here temporarily to visit her daughter. When she left a few weeks later, I had been determined to keep her out of my mind and desires. No easy task. Rubi Belta had captured them both. My *mala* didn't know she was not staying.

I went into my systems, finalizing the order of the items she requested. The trees would be challenging, or more likely, impossible. Stryxia had worked very hard to rejuvenate the natural environment of our land. Introducing an alien species could be catastrophic. But perhaps there was a way to work around it. There was this "artificial tree" she spoke of, but she seemed to prefer the real one.

If I could get it for her, I would. Despite what I said, nothing was impossible. I would try to fulfill Rubi's requests. They sounded frivolous to me, but they seemed extremely important to her. And making the human females more comfortable and at home here was a reward in itself. These females were our salvation. All our hopes and futures rested with them. It was too late for me, but not for the next generation of Stryxian males hoping for mates and families and happiness. Christmas or Hanukkah or whatever they celebrated, I would do what I could to make it happen.

And I may not want to admit it, but it was for her. Rubi. The female I could never have. The female who was from Earth. She belonged there. From what I'd heard, her mate was lost in the Morr-ta war. Not only that, but her son, too. I closed my eyes, just imagining what that must've been like. The pain had to have been unbearable. And yet, here she was—out here on Stryxia for Andi and Xarik. There was nothing about Rubi that I didn't admire.

I was about to leave the shop, to take a moment and get some fresh air, when in walked a familiar face. "Hello, Arus," I said. "If you are here about the Gamo-rian converter cells, I told you I would let you know when they came in."

"I am not here about that, Rix." Arus looked grim. "There are some things Keira wants delivered from Earth for the upcoming human festivities."

I narrowed my eyes. "If it includes strings of lights, be aware that plenty have been ordered. I am letting you know right now that you are going to be recruited to make adapters to power them."

Arus' brows rose. "Consider me recruited. I take it that you have had a number of orders for this holiday season?"

"Yes." I threw up my hands. "The forms I have to fill out to try to get a tree from their planet. They're going to be denied. Of that, I'm certain."

"Ah." Arus rocked on his heels. "Somebody wants a Christmas tree, do they?"

"Rubi Belta wants one for her soon-to-be-born grandchild."

Arus nodded. "There's a type of tree that grows here on Stryxia that is similar enough to their evergreen trees. I am having one of the northern rangers deliver one for Keira as a surprise." He cracked a real grin. "She was lamenting the lack of a Christmas tree."

I rubbed my chin. "How similar are they exactly?"

Arus shrugged. "I have not seen one in person, but I saw images. They are cone-shaped, green, and have short bristles on their limbs. They grow in abundance near the northern axis point," he said. "It is worth it, I think. Even if the tree is not exactly the same, females appreciate thoughtful gestures."

Mind made up, I nodded. "Do you think your ranger would be willing to bring a few more? I'll pay him well."

Arus shrugged again. "I don't see why not. He thought I was daft for wanting a tree delivered in exchange for the custom navigation unit I built for his transport, but I thought it a fair trade, considering how happy it will make Keira."

I did not roll my eyes, although the urge was there. Arus, gruff and big as he was, was beyond smitten with his female. And the feeling was clearly mutual.

"Oh," I said, remembering what Rubi had said. "What do they smell like?"

"Smell?"

"Yes." I waved my hand in front of my nose. "Do they have a distinct odor?"

Now it was Arus' turn to look at me like I was daft. "I do not know what they smell like."

I shook my head. "Ah, it matters not. They want trees in their homes, they get trees."

Arus tapped the counter. "You are getting it now," he said. "Here is Keira's order." He handed me the list on his slim lightboard.

Again, I would put in the order, but I didn't know what most of it was. *Candy canes.* I shook my head. "These females are strange creatures."

Arus grinned wider. "You need to find yourself one, my friend. I heard that there was some connection between you and Andi's daughter."

I took a deep breath and released it slowly. "You heard wrong. There is no connection at all. That female has no intention of staying here. What would be the point of spending time with her?"

Arus cocked his head. "You might be able to change her mind."

I had gone this long in my life without a mate. I would not disgrace myself by behaving like a youngling, chasing females around. "I have no interest in such things," I said. "I am quite content on my own."

Arus laughed. "All right, then. Also, do you have any idea when the Gamorian converter cells will be coming in?"

I couldn't tell if he was joking or serious. "I already

told you, Arus. I will send you a message when they arrive."

"Right, right." He nodded and headed for the door. "What about a general timeframe—"

"Goodbye, Arus."

The oversized engineer nodded and made his way out. At least the tree issue was taken care of. If this plant could be acquired, it would save me an enormous number of applications—and rejections—to get Earth trees delivered to our planet.

CHAPTER
Three

Rubi

"YOU REALLY TRIED to order a Christmas tree?" Andromeda chuckled as she arranged the toys I'd bought for the baby on a shelf. "What did he say?"

"He complained." I sat in the rocking chair that I had packed up and had sent to Stryxia with me. I'd nursed Andromeda in that chair many years ago. Now, she would rock her baby in it. "But he said he'd look into it. He wanted to know the exact species of tree I wanted, for some forms he had to fill out. I don't know what species of tree we got. There were different ones." I shrugged. "Some were pokier than others. There was that one that had us all in bandages after decorating it. That was awful."

"The blue spruce."

I shook my head. "*Why* did we get that one?"

"Ricky thought the dusty blue color looked nice," my daughter said quietly.

"Ah." My heart still squeezed when I thought or spoke about my son. "He loved blue when he was a boy."

Andromeda nodded. "And outer space."

"Like his father." My husband was another subject that would always pull. Time had passed, as had the acute pain and grief that had been part of me in the aftermath of loss. I'd be forever changed, but with the help of time, work, and a lot of therapy, I'd found my balance again, and with it, joy. Part of that joy was being here, with my daughter as she started her own family with Xarik.

The sound of nails clicking on the floor heralded the arrival of Haggis, Andromeda's dog, whom I'd cared for after she'd been abducted. There were no words for the fear I'd known when Haggis had been found wandering the streets alone, without his owner. I scratched behind his ear and he leaned into my touch with a grunt. "Are you ready for a baby brother or sister?" I murmured to him. I missed him, now that he lived here on Stryxia with Andromeda.

"I think he knows." Andromeda knelt down beside Haggis and rubbed his furry chest. "He follows me around everywhere."

"He's a good boy." I leaned down and kissed the top of his head, earning a quick lick in return.

"Mom, I just want to say, I don't need a tree," Andromeda said. "You're here, and that's all I want."

I leaned over and hugged her over the dog, sandwiching Haggis in the middle. He didn't seem to mind it, having the opportunity to bathe both of us in his kisses. "Honey, those words are the greatest gift a mother could ever receive. Thank you."

Andromeda leaned back, looking at me with a serious expression. "I still think you should consider moving here."

I shook my head. We'd had this conversation before. "You know they want women who can bond with Stryxian males and continue the species. I don't qualify for that."

"They would make an exception," she said. "You *know* they would."

"I don't want to be an exception," I said firmly. "Andromeda, I've come to peace with the past. I live a good life. A full life. Don't worry about me."

She looked down, frowning. "I hate thinking about you all alone."

I snorted. "I have a life, daughter. Despite what you may think." Sort of. It involved a lot of books and cups of tea, yoga classes and a part-time job that kept me busy. Not needing to worry about money, thanks to Xarik's ridiculous generosity, offered breathing room I hadn't known since before my husband died.

"There are a lot of males here your age," Andromeda persisted. "I specifically remember you making eyes with Rix. You two were giving off sparks."

"An illusion, I'm afraid," I said, frowning at the

memory of our last conversation. "He is definitely *not* interested."

"Well, then we can introduce you to—"

I held up a hand to stop her. "Honey, you can't force these things. I'm fine. I can, and will, visit often. You focus that busy energy of yours on the baby that's coming in a few weeks."

Andromeda let the topic shift and we thankfully veered away from the subject of my love life. Hardly a subject worth lingering on. Not when there were so many amazing things happening in her life right now. I set aside thoughts of Rixen as I had so many other things, with a wistful sigh and a sweep of my hair. He wasn't going to take up one more minute in my head.

CHAPTER
Four

Rixen

IT HAD BEEN eight *lumis* since Rubi had come into my shop to place her order. That isn't to say I hadn't seen her. My eyes had become attuned to seeking out her distinctive red hair. Even when I wasn't aware that I was looking for her, anything flashing that dark shade made my attention snap to it. When it wasn't her, my chest compressed with disappointment. For her part, she did a fine job of staying away from me. My glimpses were rare.

She had to be taking a different route around Trakia, since the fastest route took her right past my shop to get to the main shopping area. I did not like the thought that she was purposefully trying to avoid me. I must have offended her a great deal, although I still wasn't sure what I said to cause the offense. She *wasn't* staying on Stryxia. And yes, that frustrated me. It prevented me from following my instincts and getting closer to her. There was no greater misery for a Stryxian male than to be separated from his mate. Physically and emotionally, it was torture. Or so I'd heard.

However, Rubi was the least of my worries.

I strode down the center lane, hastily. It was early morning. The sky was a streaky purple as one of the suns warmed the village with light. A light mist rose from the stones I walked on. Most of Trakia still slept. *I* would be sleeping if circumstances were normal. But they were not.

I'd received an alert in the night that one of my transports—the one carrying all the humans' holiday orders, of course—had lost a rear drive thruster when entering the atmosphere and had landed in the Sanrous Plains. The operator, a Rulgan male who was usually reliable, if a bit jumpy, had sent a brief, confusing message about noises in the dark, and had abandoned the ship. He'd sent for a small transport to pick him up and that was the last I'd heard from him.

My transport was presumably still sitting there, exposed, in the uninhabited plains that were still rejuvenating after many lifeless years. I had exhausted the rest of the night trying to hire a new operator who would retrieve it, but to no avail. Enough absurd superstitions existed about abandoned ships to ward off the few operators who were available at short notice.

I fumed as I strode toward my shop, which located only a few blocks from my residence. Ordinarily, I liked the walk. Today, it felt terribly long. All I had to do was post a notice that I wouldn't be open today before I returned home and set out on a journey I had not anticipated.

I was tired, annoyed, and vowed to not hire that Rulgan male again, no matter the explanation, since it looked like I'd be retrieving the transport ship myself, and repairing the drive enough to limp it back to Trakia. The Christmas holiday that the humans were so excited about was five *lumis* away.

My thoughts were not on the walkway in front of me, otherwise I would have heard the sound of someone walking the other way. I rounded a corner and nearly walked straight into a beautiful human female walking a hairy, brown creature that let out a noise like, "ruff," and wagged a shaggy tail.

"Oh!" Rubi Belta stopped suddenly, yanking small white things out of her ears. "I didn't...I'm sorry." Her full red hair was pulled up into a messy bun. Before my eyes, red splotches appeared on her neck and chest, above the full rise of her breasts. She wore a sleeveless shirt and baggy pants, both in black.

The animal, known throughout Trakia as a *dog*, was famous with the human females. They all cooed over him and he appeared to enjoy the attention. The creature had a name—Haggis. I gazed down at the thing that wiggled at the end of his leash, with clear pleasure shining in his big brown eyes. I absently patted the *dog's* head. My senses were overwhelmed with the female. She smelled like morning and flowers. Her skin was flushed.

"My apologies, Rubi," I said, bowing my head. "I was not paying attention to my path."

"I was listening to music," she said, holding up the small white things. She was working to collect herself. A cool expression fell over her features, wiping away the surprise and fluster. "I didn't hear you."

"Do you often walk this beast in the early morning?" I asked.

"Yes, I do," she replied. "I like mornings. They clear my head." Her brow dropped. "And he's not a beast. He's a very sweet dog."

My gaze dropped to the dog, who panted happily up at me. "Of course." I bent down and scratched his chin, causing him to close his eyes and lean into my touch. "He is a pleasant creature."

Now her brows rose. "I never see *you* out this early, Rixen."

There was no missing the slightly accusatory tone, as if I'd purposefully plotted to unsettle her morning walk with my presence. "I have a disabled transport out on the plains," I explained. "I need to get out there and bring it in."

Concern softened her expression. "What happened?"

I waved a hand. "Drive thruster went and the operator abandoned it." I lacked time and energy, but I had to clear the air with Rubi while I had her face-to-face. "Rubi, I upset you the last time we spoke. Would you enlighten me as to what I said that offended you?"

She blinked, as if surprised by my blunt question. "I

believe you implied that because I'm not here to breed, I'm a nuisance and shouldn't be here."

I nearly fell backwards. "I said no such thing."

"No, but you said the females who stay are the ones who are appreciated." Her eyes flickered with uncertainty. "I assumed you mean the ones young enough to produce babies."

I rubbed my forehead, suddenly seeing how my words could be taken that way and inwardly cursing myself for them. "I apologize for the hurt I caused you." I bowed formally. "I assure you, I do *not* consider breeding to be the worth of a female. My words were the result of frustration that your visits to Stryxia are brief." I felt myself bending toward her, even now. My eyes stung with the marker of a possible bond. If we were to give in to this and allow it to happen, my black eyes would eventually change to her dark blue color, as was the case with all Stryxian males.

"That *my* visits are brief?" She looked up at me quizzically. "But I annoy you."

I let out a rusty laugh. "Your orders occasionally annoy me. You do not."

"Oh." Color rose on her cheeks again. She looked distinctly flustered. "You wish my visits were longer?"

My wings flared. The tiny hairs on the inner side of them could release pheromones that either augmented or attempted to correct a situation. They could sooth stress or enhance excitement, among other things, and they did so without my control. I hoped they weren't releasing an aphrodisiac at that moment. It would not be appropriate. But still, I had no reason to be vague with her. "I wish your visits were to Earth and this was your home." There. I said it.

She stared at me. "Rixen, are you saying that you like me?"

"Yes. Is there a clearer way to say it?" I frowned. "But I cannot indulge those thoughts. Your home is on Earth. I accept that."

"Um." Haggis was growing impatient with this delay in his walk. He whined and wound his leash around Rubi. "I wasn't expecting you to say that."

"I was not expecting this conversation." I glanced past her to where my shop lay dark and unopened. "It appears I have once again upset you."

I moved to walk on, but she stopped me with a hand to my arm. Her touch seared through my shirt to the skin. "No, you didn't. I'm floored."

"You are what?"

"I'm…surprised. A little overwhelmed."

I nodded, accepting that Rubi's feelings did not match mine. "I see. Good day, Rubi Bel—"

"Rixen, I really like Stryxia," she said, cutting me off. "My daughter is happy here, and I'm about to have a grandchild."

"Yes?"

She licked her lips. "I'm not good at this," she muttered, then drew in a deep breath. "I like you too, and would like to get to know you better." Her words came out in a rush, making my translator implant delay in processing her words.

My throat tightened. Her dark blue eyes were turbu-
lent, unsure, cautious, but also hopeful. Beautifully,
openly hopeful. "I would like that." My voice sounded
like gravel to my ears. "When I return, perhaps we can
share a meal."

She smiled, making her eyes sparkle. "How long
will you be?"

"I will be back by tonight."

A new expression lit her face. "Hey, I know this is
short notice and you can say no, but maybe I can go
with you to the transport? If it's not too far. I've always
wanted to see more of this planet. It could be fun."

My mind immediately went through the logistics of
how that would work. Her straddling the *sandspitter*
behind me. Her warm thighs wrapped around mine for
the duration of the journey to the ship. Spending the
day with her as I did the repairs and showing her the
beauty of my planet outside of the Trakia village. I
could not say no to this female. Something had sparked
to life in my chest that mirrored what I saw in Rubi's
eyes—hope.

It was one day. A few hours to get out to the ship.
Another couple to fix the drive thruster, then a fast ride
back to Trakia's central hangar. "Very well."

CHAPTER
Five

Rubi

I HURRIED to Andromeda and Xarik's home with a very happy Haggis leading the way. He was eager for his breakfast and to see his favorite lady. The dog had been very doting on my daughter during her pregnancy. Even though he loved our morning walks, he liked to stay by Andromeda's side. I let myself in, not expecting to see anyone up, but Andromeda yawned and waddled across the central room in an enormous nightgown. "Morning, Mom." Haggis bounded over to her and sniffed thoroughly, starting at the toes. "Hiya, baby boy," she crooned, kissing his head and scratching his neck. "How was your walk?"

I didn't know if she was asking me or the dog, but I was bursting at the seams to tell her what had just happened between Rixen and me, so I launched into it. "I am going on a road trip with Rixen," I announced.

"And I don't have much time, so I'm just telling you what I'm doing. I'll be gone all day."

She looked up, blinking the sleep from her eyes. "You're what?"

I held up a hand. "I'm not asking permission, so don't even start."

"I'm not..." Andromeda shook her head. "Can you just tell me what happened?"

I gave her a brief rundown of my near collision with him and the conversation that followed. I wasn't sure how coherent I was, being a little out of breath.

Xarik walked in during the part where I explained about the transport breaking down. He'd missed the beginning part of it where I told Andromeda about my misunderstanding of Rixen's words and what he said to me. "Rix's ship is disabled in the plains?" Xarik's brow furrowed. "I'll send an escort with him to retrieve it."

"No!" both Andromeda and I said simultaneously.

"Hmm." His eyes widened. "What did I miss?"

Andromeda leaned a hip against the sofa. "Rix has finally admitted that he's sweet on my mom and they're going to the transport ship together today. Alone."

Xarik, the sweetie, looked dumbfounded for a moment before his brain caught up. He held up a finger with a nod. "Ah. I see. And it's about time. Rix's energy is always intense when you come for a visit, Rubi. Glad that's no longer a secret."

"Really?" I crossed my arms. "You're my son-in-law. You couldn't have let *me* in on that secret?"

He grinned, showing off dimples, and came by to

kiss my cheek before continuing on to the kitchen. "I also didn't tell *him* that *your* energy is a hot, chaotic mess when you return from visiting his shop."

"Well." Heat warmed my cheeks. "Hardly something you should be noticing, Xarik."

"Impossible to miss," he called over his shoulder. "Have a nice time in the Sanrous Plains.

"I will," I said to him, then turned to Andromeda with a wince, having a sudden wave of second thoughts. "Maybe this is a bad idea."

"If it is, you'll know by the end of the day." She ushered me toward the door. "You're not going to stand that male up. Give him a chance."

I nodded, pushing away the doubts. "I haven't done anything impulsive in forever."

"Then you're overdue," she said. "Go. Give me a full report in the morning. Actually, no. A redacted report will do."

"You don't think I'm going to—" I cut off and frowned at Andromeda. "It's a first date, for heaven's sake. Shame on you."

She laughed. "Have fun, Mom. *Allow yourself* to have fun. You deserve it, after everything."

The way she said it, filled with years of knowledge, made my eyes well up. She was right, my dear daughter. That after everything—so much loss, grief, healing—it was okay to live. To see what happens next. "I think I will," I said, then wagged my finger at her. "Don't even think about having that baby today."

She laughed and ran a hand over her belly. "Bye, Mom," she said as I headed back out.

I stopped briefly at my cottage to change into fresh clothes and grab a few things in a pack. I wasn't even sure what to bring on a day trip with a Stryxian male. I was used to things like a wallet, keys, etc., but I didn't need any of that here. Still, I didn't know how to go anywhere *without* bringing a bag of stuff with me, so I threw an extra sweatshirt, some random stuff like tissues and lip balm into a shoulder bag. I hit the bathroom and headed out. I hoped Rixen hadn't changed his mind and left without me.

The directions to his home were easy to follow since Trakia's layout wasn't complex. The road led me to a row of large dwellings. They had steep-pitched roofs and ample windows. The one that was Rixen's looked three stories tall with a large grove of trees behind it and a massive garage. Nerves jangled in my belly as I approached the front door. I raised my hand to knock but it instantly slid open.

He stood on the other side, looking mildly surprised to see me there. "You came."

"Yes." I glanced past him, into the spacious room beyond. "Was I supposed to change my mind?"

"I wondered." He ran a hand through his hair. "I mean, no. Please come in."

I followed him inside. His furnishings were deep and rich in color, made of natural things—wood, stone, metal. There was an abundance of seating, unique lights, and the smell of leather. "I love your house," I said, taking in the deeply lived-in feel of his place. It had the sense of someone who had been alone for a long time and settled in to a single life. My small apartment probably had the same vibe.

"Thank you." He stood there looking unsure of what to do. He seemed thrown off by having a woman in his house, but soon recovered. "The vehicle is back here. May I take your bag?"

"Sure. Thanks." I handed him my bag, which I now thought of as my emotional support bag, and stuck my hands in my pockets. I wore the same loose pants from the morning, but had changed into a fresh top and layered on a hooded jacket. The most common ground vehicles in Trakia were these motorcycle-ish things called *sandspitters* that had propulsion underneath instead of wheels, and were ridden astride. They had high sides and a windshield that came up and over the riders, but there was still wind.

Sure enough, that was the vehicle he led me to. It sat in the garage, or rather, small hangar, in gleaming tan. "Now *this* is a beast," I said, taking in the large vehicle.

"This is an older model, but it will get us there quickly." He secured my bag in a compartment and handed me a thick, clear ring. "Let me put this on you."

The ring was soft and had a break on one side. He opened the circle and fitted it around my neck, like a collar. My hands immediately went for it and I found that it had sealed. "What is this?" I asked nervously.

"It's for the sand and dirt, and this..." He pulled a thick, hooded cloak from the wall. "Is for the wind."

"Oh." I let him drape the cloak over my shoulders, then watched as he pulled a clear ring around his own neck.

A panel on one side of the vehicle slid open as he approached it. He threw one leg astride. He looked terribly hot. He jerked a thumb to the smooth seat behind him. "Get on."

I swallowed with effort. My throat was suddenly dry. "Okay." I made my way over and carefully stepped up to the unfamiliar vehicle. Following his lead, but with perhaps a little less grace, I got my leg over the seat, and for the first time in my life, I knew what it felt like to sit on a motorcycle, or maybe a horse. It was a wide seat but not terribly long. There wasn't much space for the two of us with Rixen's large body and wings, which he kept tucked close to his back. The fronts of my thighs slid behind his, sealing us together. I shivered at the inevitable press of everything between my legs to his hips, ass, legs.

For a moment, neither of us did anything. I think the sudden intimate contact was a surprise, and perhaps a little more than either of us had bargained for. "Um," I said. "This is cozy."

"I rarely travel by land vehicle," he said. "This is all I have." He sounded apologetic and a little strained.

My nervousness was making me desperately try to come up with a joke, but good sense told me this wasn't the time for one. "Why aren't we flying?" I asked.

He looked over his shoulder with a rueful grin. "The distance is too far for these wings to carry me, let alone another person. If you would like to go for a short flight one of these days, I am happy to comply."

I smiled and wrapped my arms around his waist. "I would like that."

"Very well. Now, keep your hands off your face," he said.

"How com—?" I was beginning to ask, but he turned on the vehicle and instantly, the clear ring around my neck activated with a hum. A moment later, a translucent bubble grew from the clear base and encapsulated my head. The "helmet" was very slim, and by that I mean it hugged close to the contours of my face, following my features, so that there was about an inch of clearing between my skin and the transparent mask that would keep the wind off of my face.

I touched the surface tentatively and felt like I was pressing against taut plastic wrap.

"I told you," he said. "If your finger was in there, it would have glitched the device." A shiny bubble had also appeared around his head. Then the quiet engine began and the *sandspitter* eased out of the hangar and into the open space beyond.

Behind Rixen's home was an open roadway. I had to assume the purpose of it was in case the settlement needed to be quickly evacuated, because the roadway ran behind all the houses in Rixen's neighborhood. No one else was driving on it, however. Just us. And I could see the need for these high-tech helmets. Despite the shielding on the front and sides of the *sandspitter*, there was a fair amount of wind pouring around the edges.

Still, it was a *fun* vehicle and unlike anything I'd ridden on before. I resisted the urge to let out a whoop as we passed out of Trakia and into the open land, where only the faintest trace of a road existed. No *corsic* tile stones lined a wide lane here. This "road" was just a slightly different shade of brown, packed soil.

The miles flew past and I watched the landscape shift and change. In some respects, it wasn't too different from Earth. A lot of effort had been put into plantings in and around Trakia village, but out here, the land was still rebuilding and different. Hills rolled by. Mountains snaggled along the horizon. There were groves of new forest, tracts of grass and shrubbery, and an occasional stream winding by.

The trees made it clear that I was *definitely* on a planet other than my own. Some of them grew at confounding angles. Their foliage was different colors and shapes. Some didn't look like trees at all, but rather, rock formations.

I leaned into the broad, warm body in front of me. Rixen was a solid wall of muscle. My arms felt comfortable around him. He didn't speak much, but when he did, it was to point out an old landmark.

That pile of rubble over there was once a gathering place for artists.

Vigrets *infested the sands past that ridge. Mean little beasts.*

There used to be a lake over there. The water was purple and swimming in it made your scales shine like glass.

I listened to these short descriptions with pleasure. It was obvious he was very fond of his home world, and proud of it. I could appreciate how heartbreaking it must have been to see it destroyed. I, too, had had my world destroyed. I tightened my grip around Rixen's middle, feeling like we *did* have something in common —we'd risen from rubble and rebuilt our lives.

We stopped for a break in a grove of trees where, Rixen explained, there had once been a spring that supplied a nearby village with water. It was now a small pool, surrounded by lush greenery, and it looked like something out of an enchanted story. The surrounding forest gave us just enough space and privacy for quick pee breaks, and then we were back on the *sandspitter*.

The rest of the ride went quickly. Rixen talked a little bit more. The further away we traveled from Trakia, the more he loosened up. Instead of just pointing out land-marks, he spoke of his personal connections to the places we passed. There were many ruins out here, evidence of the civilization that had once flourished. But with his explanations, I could envision what Stryxia had been like before the Morr-ta war.

It was very obvious when we entered the area known as the Sanrous Plains. The land flattened. The ground was either sand or covered in thick, waving grasses that undulated like a single, fluid mass in the wind. It was beautiful and desolate, and it appeared endless.

"The grass is new," he said. "This was fully a desert until our atmosphere could hold enough moisture for regular rainfall. We should see to ship soon."

While I would be sad to be done with this part of the trip, my thighs ached from sitting astride for so long. In the distance, a dark shape shimmered. The cargo ship was large and blocky—nothing like the sleek battleships that were used in the war. "Do you do this often?" I asked.

"Bring females to crashed cargo ships? No." His cheek lifted in a smile. "First time."

"*That* was obvious," I quipped, earning me a chuckle. "Do you frequently journey out to repair broken-down ships?"

"No. The operators have extensive tools and parts, and they do not abandon the vehicles. They call for assistance or have the ship do a self-repair sequence. This operator took one of the ship's small transports—usually used for emergency evacuations—and fled."

"What caused him to do that?" I asked.

He shrugged. "His message was garbled. Something spooked him. I cannot imagine what. There is nothing out here. Then again, he is not Stryxian. Some species have unique superstitions," he replied. "All I know is that I will *not* hire him back."

As we grew nearer and nearer, the enormity of the dark gray cargo ship was revealed. It didn't look damaged. It sat on the plain, landing gear intact, as if landed there purposefully. We passed into its shadow, as the midday light blazed down. "What do you think is wrong with it?"

Rixen stopped the *sandspitter* directly beside the hulking ship. "Hopefully nothing too difficult to fix." He climbed off and stretched, then extended his hand. "Coming?"

CHAPTER
Six

Rixen

RUBI GAZED up at the ship with an open mouth and wide eyes. From down here, it was big. To a human, it would be imposing and overwhelming. The hull was dark brown, but stained darker in places where it burned in hot atmospheres and was singed by space debris. A few sections had been replaced, but these were normal aspects to a cargo ship that saw a lot of use. All the glitches and issues had been worked out, making this ship smooth-running and a reliable unit in my small, six-ship fleet that ferried cargo to and from various ports in the galaxy.

Earth was a new addition to my transport runs. Not the most profitable, but vitally important. Keeping the human females content on Stryxia was essential for the future of my species, and in truth, I adored seeing young ones running about the lanes and streets again.

Hearing their voices made my soul happy. It gave me hope for the future of my kind.

"How do we…" She waved her hand. "Get on it?"

I fished a small black screen from my coat's inside pocket and entered the transport's owner access code. "Like this."

The ship made a loud creaking sound. A huge portion of the hull released with a hiss and an expulsion of cool, pressurized air as it slowly lowered on massive hinges. Rubi watched with the same awe that she had when we approached the ship. The opening that was produced could have fit her entire cottage. The massive door landed on the ground with a thunderous clang.

"That's a big door," she said.

I laughed. "The smaller entrance is way up there." I pointed to a door halfway up the side, which was what we would be using if the ship were in a normal hangar with a lift or overpass to walk onto. "This is not the usual way to board a cargo vessel." I climbed on to the cargo bay door, which now lay out before us like a ramp for giants. It was as thick as she was tall. I squatted and reached down for her. "Let me help you up."

Rubi held up her arms and grasped my shoulders, as I fit my hands around her waist. She was lush and soft, with curves that made my mouth water. I lifted her up to stand in front of me. She didn't let go of my shoulders immediately, but stood there, flushed and breathless, as I held her.

I couldn't bring myself to release her, either. After

that long ride with her legs around mine, my pants were feeling too tight and my wings naturally arched around her in an ancient gesture of protection. I blinked, trying to rid myself of the burning in my eyes.

"Are you okay?" she asked, brow furrowing. "It looks like your eyes are bothering you."

"The dust," I said gruffly. "I am fine."

"But you still have your helmet on."

I removed one of my hands from her waist and pressed the center of the neck ring. It shimmered and disappeared. "Right there," I said, pressing the same point on her headpiece, eager to change the subject. "It automatically engages when the *sandspitter* is activated, but it needs to be manually turned off."

Almost reluctantly, she slid her hands off my shoulders. She pulled the neck piece off and looped it over an arm. "Good to know."

I didn't want to break contact with her. The thought of it felt physically uncomfortable. If I was still looking for a clear sign that my *mala* had identified her as my mate, it was this pull, this intense draw I felt toward her. It had been present before, whenever I saw her. But now, with the two of us alone, it roared at me to take what was mine. Were she Stryxian, there would be no conversation, no gentle wooing. I would take her and we would indulge the urgings of our *malas*. We would already be bonded mates by now.

Only, Rubi wasn't a Stryxian female, and, as all Stryxian males had learned, humans needed to be introduced to the notion of bonding differently. It alarmed them, sometimes. I understood how that could be, in a society where the *mala* didn't exist. Partners *chose* to be together, rather than it being a thing that simply *was*.

Instead, I shifted to her side, rested my hand on the small of her back, and guided her to the yawning opening. "Allow me to show you the AX-12 Space Runner. It comes equipped with a full hold capable of transporting three-point-two cubic *dekaliks* of cargo at nine-point-five clicks through deep space..." I babbled on about the ship, a pointless and absurd thing to do. No one—not even I—needed to hear this information voiced aloud.

The truth was, I was nervous. We were out here alone. Just Rubi, me, and the quiet hiss of the wind over the grasses of the plain. Suddenly, I didn't know what to do. I didn't know how to act. This was about as far out of my skill set as it got.

She laid a hand on my arm. "I'm not going to bite you, Rixen."

"I know," I said, thankful she cut off my rambling monologue.

"I'd break my teeth on your scales."

I laughed. "You would. And I am far too tough and salty."

Her eyes twinkled as she gazed up at me. "Oh, I bet you're actually pretty soft and sweet under all this."

My pulse began to tick faster. My wings shivered and I tucked them as close to my body as I could to avoid any interesting pheromones being released. Those chemicals had discernible scents, and human females were well aware of their powers. "Nonsense, female." I smiled down at her. "What you see is what you get."

She arched one brow. "Sold."

I suspected Rubi was flirting with me. That was what they called it when a female engaged in banter with certain insinuations. I couldn't be sure that she wasn't just teasing, or enjoying seeing me thrown off balance, but we had already admitted an interest in one another. Rubi was outgoing and friendly with everyone. She was bold and affectionate and fierce. I had not observed her being coy or manipulative, so I concluded that what I perceived was what it appeared to be: *flirting*.

I cleared my throat and decided to give this flirting business a try. "Are you sure? I offer no returns or exchanges."

Rubi laughed, loud and clear. The lush sound echoed through the quiet cargo hold. "Nice, Rixen." She leaned close to me. The side of her breast brushed my arm. "Neither do I."

I took in her gentle, sweet scent. Her soft hair smelled like something out of my fantasies. I held off the urge to drag her into my arms and taste her sweet, pink lips. "I have never done this before," I murmured.

"What?" she asked.

"This." I gestured to the two of us. "Talked so with a female."

"That's a shame. You're good at it."

"Am I?"

"Yes." She looked around at the large cargo hold,

about half-filled with large crates and containers. "And I hate to end it, but where is the bathroom? My bladder is screaming at me."

"This way." It was a relief to turn my attention to something other than the alluring female beside me. I had a ship to repair and get back to Trakia—hopefully before nightfall—and that wouldn't happen if I stood around flirting with Rubi for the next few hours.

I led her from the cargo hold to a passageway leading to the control center of the ship. Here, there was a chamber dedicated to bodily needs, including a full body cleaning and decontamination system and personal waste disposal.

"Thanks." She slipped inside with an audible sigh and the door shut behind her.

I let out a sigh myself, from the sensations riding me. I had to get my head together. The control center of the ship was directly adjacent. Rubi would see me in there when she emerged, so there was no need to hover at the door. I entered the control room, a half-circle with a domed front that featured a wide window to the outside, and sat at the main terminal. It was in the center of the room, which had five terminals total. Only one operator was needed to fly the ship, but there were times I sent a full crew for security of valuable cargo. String lights and random Earth items didn't classify as valuable—at least, not to the types who would consider attacking the ship for its cargo—so one operator was all that had been needed. Or, so I'd thought.

"What are you doing?" Rubi asked, coming to stand

beside me.

"Running a diagnostic," I replied, fingers working over the touch screen. "To find out what happened to the stabilizer so I can pinpoint what needs repair."

"Ah." She sat in a different chair, gazing through the huge window to the scene outside. I glanced up to see her simply observing. Her face and body were relaxed. From our height at the front of the ship, the vista was huge and stunning. The light played on the grass and along the horizon. I looked back to my work, pleased that she was not a female who needed constant chatter and entertainment. I was not a male who could offer that, even when I was younger.

As the diagnostic ran, I switched to the operator's logs, which should explain what he'd experienced and why he'd left. Oddly enough, the Rulgan male had left voice recordings, not text logs. I synched the earpiece I wore—to translate Rubi's words—to the interface and listened.

The operator logged the stabilizer issues. They appeared when he passed the ship through Stryxia's atmosphere. He couldn't bring the ship to the Trakia port, and so, took it down here, in the Sanrous Plains. The male's voice was calm. His entries were brief, but clear and detailed enough for me to follow.

The Rulgan male had run the same diagnostic I had, with the intention of fixing the stabilizer and bringing the ship to Trakia as planned. But with each successive entry, his voice became tighter, frantic. He was hearing things in the ship that frightened him. He'd armed himself and attempted to find the source of the noises, but they skittered away. When he arrived at the stabilizer unit, deep within the guts of the ship, he described it as gnawed on and destroyed. Unrepairable. He saw something moving back there—a dark shape scurrying away and a sound like a growl.

The last entry was what he'd sent me, which I'd heard at the shop. A terrified voice, barely comprehensible, saying that he'd taken one of the small getaway transports and fled the planet. He was forfeiting his fee. He was afraid for his life.

I leaned back in my seat, frowning, as the last log finished. A knot of dread curled in my gut, along with the knowledge that I should *not* have brought Rubi here.

"You look upset," Rubi said. She'd swiveled her chair to face me. "What's wrong?"

I shook my head. "The operator did not just frivolously leave. He believed something was on this ship."

Her brows drew together. "What kind of something?"

"It frightened him enough to fear for his life," I replied.

"Hmm. We've been on this ship for a while," she said. "I haven't heard anything. Do you think whatever it was might have left?"

I tapped a finger absently on my armrest. "Perhaps."

Just then, a sound scraped through the ship like a groaning twist of metal. We froze, eyes locking. "Or not."

CHAPTER
Seven

Rubi

RIXEN RETURNED TO THE SCREEN, fingers working over commands with ease and confidence. "Ship censors should pick up where that sound came from," he said. "Ah. There it is. This is pretty far inside the ship. Way back in the maintenance sector."

"Well, then that's where we're going," I said. "Let's go."

"No. *You* are not to leave this room," he said. "Under any circumstances. I will go alone."

I almost rolled my eyes. "I knew you were going to say that."

"I mean it."

"I know you do," I said. "But I'm going with you."

He closed his eyes, as if digging for patience. "It is not safe."

"I know. That's why I'm going." I rose, planting

hands on my hips. "When is the last time you had to fight someone, or something? Do you even know how to use a blaster?"

"I fought in the Morr-ta war," he said, rising to his feet.

"Okay." My voice hardened. "My husband and son died in it. I lived alone, caring for a young daughter in a city that was in chaos. Do you think I have never had to defend myself?"

"This is different," he said, stepping closer to me. "This is no weak human male to fend off unwanted advances from. This is possibly an alien creature with capabilities we are not aware of."

I didn't enjoy being underestimated, but I could see how it could happen. I was an older lady with a few extra pounds and a sassy attitude, who didn't look menacing at all. And Stryxian males had a thing about protecting us. Sure, we were smaller than them, and we didn't have wings or scales, but we were tough. I had a twenty-two-year-old sleep shirt that was in tatters, but which *I still wore,* printed with flowers and butterflies and words in a script font that read: "This bitch will fuck you up." Not the classiest of phrases, but I wasn't always the classiest of women.

I smiled at him. "I'm going with you and I'd like a blaster."

"You know how to use one?"

"Yes." I stepped closer, narrowing the space between us to inches. "After what my daughter went through, it seemed prudent to have a refresher. Before that, I had training in various firearms and martial arts." I was pretty sure by the flash of confusion that his translator gave him a strange definition of "martial arts," but I was in no mood to find this amusing.

His eyes narrowed. "Is that so?"

"Yes. We were at war with aliens and we weren't sure we'd win. I didn't plan to go down without a fight and the city offered free lessons on self-defense and how to handle blasters, in case Earth was occupied. I *can* defend myself." Then I pushed the envelope and probably shouldn't have. "Can *you?*"

His nostrils flared. His arms came around me and yanked me against him, making the slight space between us disappear. "Yes. I fought as a warrior. Morrta died by my hand," he said. "I will allow no harm to come to you."

My hands and chest pressed to his. My heart beat fast against his chest as I let out a sigh. "Look, despite our bluster, we're both rusty. Together we might stand a chance against whatever is lurking in this ship, but not alone."

"I don't like this."

"Neither do I," I said. "But we're going to find out what this is together."

Those black eyes moved over me with hunger and a proprietary light. "Rubi, you will stay behind me at all times. You will *not* put yourself in direct danger. Is that clear?"

I felt myself bristling at the authoritative tone in his voice, but it was also weirdly sexy. Rixen was clearly worried about me. More worried about me than he was about himself. "Very clear," I said. "Now, where are those weapons?"

Muttering a curse I couldn't quite make out, he opened a wall compartment and withdrew two basic-looking blasters. They were very similar to the kinds I had taken training in.

He handed one to me with a stern look. "These are only for emergencies. Let's hope we don't have to use them."

"I couldn't agree more."

Rixen pursed his lips, clearly displeased by the entirety of this business. "Remember what I said," he growled. "Got it?"

I nodded. "Stay behind you and don't shoot anything."

"Especially where we are going," he added. "The maintenance corridors are where all the specialized equipment is. Hitting something down there could blow up the ship or strand us a lot longer than we expected."

"No problem," I said. "Lead the way."

We wound through the hallways of the cargo ship. It was as bare bones as you got on one of these vessels. Lighting was simple and bright. The walls were metal and loud as we walked. Being down here was like a maze. Rixen seemed to know his way around, which was a good thing because I would've been lost the moment we left the control room.

Most of the ship was comprised of cargo space, so

we didn't have to walk that far to arrive in the area clearly designated to the guts of the ship. Corridors became narrower and the ceilings lower. Vast ropes of tubes and wires covered the surfaces. Blinking panels that I guessed were high-tech circuit boards stood upright in large racks, radiating heat. Rixen slowed his pace. He held his free hand out behind him, signaling for me to stay back. We were getting closer. Somewhere ahead of us was the sound of electricity spitting, as if arcing from severed wires.

I gripped my blaster and *really* hoped I didn't need to use it down here. Rixen was right—there was no place to shoot where we wouldn't hit something important. But if whatever we encountered tried to attack, we'd have to risk it.

Rixen stopped. He turned and gestured towards the ceiling. "There," he whispered.

I saw immediately what he referred to. A massive twist of wires looked as if they had been chewed through. The section was frayed away, revealing the source of the electrical zapping sound I'd heard.

But more alarming than that was the small creature crouched *inside* this sparking mass. It was dark red and trying to blend into the shadows around it. "What is that?" I hissed.

Rixen shook his head. "That species is unknown to me. But sitting behind it is the centrifuge."

"I take it that's a bad thing to shoot up?"

"Very bad." He squinted and took another step forward. "It looks almost like a..." He shook his head.

"No. I do not know what it is, but we must figure that out so we can know what to do with it. It cannot stay here. It has done enough damage already."

"You think this is the reason why the ship went down in the first place?"

He nodded. "Those wires attach to the stabilizer."

"Oh."

————

Huge, luminous yellow eyes blinked at us warily from the sparking mass, which didn't seem to bother it at all. It had long ears, similar to a rabbit, that were perked in our direction. A tiny nose twitched as it ardently sniffed at us, and I couldn't see the mouth at all. Its body shape reminded me a little of a monkey, from what I could see of it.

"It's cute," I said. "Maybe it's friendly."

"If it were friendly, my operator would not have run off in terror," he said. "It's unlikely to be open to a cuddle."

I smiled. "I'm not saying we should cuddle it. Just see if it's bitey."

Rixen sighed, shook his head, and took a gingerly step forward. "Little creature," he said quietly. "We are not here to hurt you."

A tiny blue tongue flicked out and wiped over the creature's nose. It blinked those huge eyes.

Rixen took another step forward, and it proved to be one too many. "We are here to—"

The small creature finally revealed its mouth, opened it wide, and showed off a mouthful of pointy white teeth. Its dark fur stood up on end like thousands of tiny spikes as it emitted a warning growl.

Rixen stepped away backwards, shooting me an I-told-you-so look. "It's bitey."

I shrugged. "It was worth a try."

When we were once again at a distance the creature felt comfortable with, it settled back down into its nest of sparking wires and regarded us as it had before, with big yellow eyes.

"You know we cannot repair the ship until we get rid of that thing," Rixen said.

I patted him on the shoulder. "Let's find out what that thing is first, then, shall we? You have a good database on this ship, I assume, or at least we can access Trakia's from here."

He nodded and took my hand, leading me back through the labyrinth of maintenance corridors and back to the control room.

Here, we replaced our blasters in the storage compartment and sat down.

"We could call the settlement and ask them to send a few people to help out," I said.

His brow lowered. "Trakia does not need to send out people to deal with one little…" He waved his hand in the air. "Whatever that is. I will handle it."

"How?"

"First, I will bring you back to the village," he said.

"Then I will return and deal with that creature. You need to get back. Your daughter needs you."

I opened my mouth to say that I'd just stay. That there was no point in wasting all that time and energy in bringing me back to the settlement, then coming back out, but the words faded before I uttered them.

My daughter. Amid all the excitement and mild terror, it had slipped my mind that Andi's baby was due so very soon. I *did* need to get back.

"You're right," I said. "Andi's due in a few days and I'm…"

"Say no more. The cargo can wait." He ran the backs of his fingers down my cheek. "Your daughter cannot."

I nodded, disappointed that our little trip would end like this. I had been looking forward to sitting with him as he worked, chatting, and then enjoying an evening ride back to the village. Something was changing between the two of us. Changing rapidly. The way he looked at me, the way my heart beat when he was nearby, and the way my skin burned when he touched me, even accidentally.

We would have more time when he returned, I told myself. I wasn't going home to Earth right away. Just the thought of what *could* happen between us made me feel nervous and excited at the same time. The ramifications were overwhelming when I let it begin to play out in my mind. Did I actually want to uproot my life and change it completely for a second chance at romance? Or did I simply like the fantasy?

I smiled, but stepped away from his touch. "Well, I guess we should get going."

He nodded, slowly dropping his hand. "Of course. This way."

We went back through passageways and into the cargo hold, which was still open. We walked down the massive ramp to where the *sandspitter* was and found it...

"What in the name of *Trall* happened here?" Rixen roared.

Pieces of the *sandspitter* were strewn all over the ground. It looked as if it had been ripped apart.

Dread shivered over my skin. I stepped closer to Rixen and wrapped my hand around his forearm. "That little creature in the maintenance corridor did *not* do this."

He went still. "No, it did not." He turned jet black eyes to me, then narrowed them on the landscape around us. There was nothing to see but grasses and some trees in the distance. Afternoon was pulling the two stars low, turning the sky to the shade of a bruise.

"Back inside, quickly," he said. "We are calling for help."

"Good idea."

"We may not get you out of here tonight." He looked apologetic. "I am sorry."

"It's fine. It's probably some hungry or scared creature that accidentally got picked up from a space station somewhere."

"Maybe," he said grimly. "I care not where it came

from. I want it out of here." He raised one dark brow at me. "All the holiday items you and the other humans ordered are in this ship. Your holiday is five days away. I promise, I will get you and this ship back to Trakia village by then so you can be there to welcome your new grandchild. He or she will have those colored lights to look at."

I placed a hand on his chest. "You know the lights are not the most important thing right now, right?"

"They matter to you," he said. "So they matter to me." His wings extended and curved around me. A warm, soothing scent filled my senses. It was a sure sign that the fine, velvety fur on the inner surface of those wings was releasing its pheromone. It wasn't meant to arouse, however. The chemical his wings gave off just then was meant to comfort and soothe me. Or rather, both of us. Stryxians were just as affected by their pheromones as those near them were.

I took a deep, relaxed breath, putting up no resistance to his wings' chemical release. My muscles unwound and I swayed a little on my feet. "Thank you, Rixen."

He steadied me with his big, strong hands, and pressed his lips to my head. "My pleasure, Rubi."

Oh boy. My heart was doing things it hadn't done in a long time and, no, it wasn't having a heart attack. So much for a sexy whirlwind romance with a hunky Stryxian. I was *falling in love* with this guy.

CHAPTER
Eight

Rixen

THIS WAS NOT GOOD. The smell of *cralium* was pungent in the air. Whatever had destroyed the *sand-spitter* had ripped its way into the power bank itself, which was no easy task. The *cralium* nodes—the power source—were well protected and deep inside the vehicle. The fact that I could smell the acetic odor of *cralium* meant it was shocking there hadn't been an explosion. It was a very unstable substance when outside of its protective nodes.

I hated the bite of fear in Rubi's voice and the tension in her eyes. I had not brought her out here so she could be afraid. My body released stress-relieving pheromones that relaxed her almost instantly. I kissed the top of her forehead, wanting to do more. Scooping her up and carrying her to the nearest bed was an idea.

A bad one, though. We had real problems. Potentially deadly problems.

"So much for a fun sightseeing trip," I muttered.

"It's not that bad," she said. "As long as whatever did that…" She pointed to the *sandspitter*. "Isn't inside *there*." She swung her finger towards the gaping-open cargo hold.

I cursed myself for leaving it open. But there were no known creatures living in the Sanrous Plains. There were no beings with that kind of destructive power on Stryxia *at all*. "Whatever did this was from off-planet. I will check the logs again to see where the operator stopped on his way from Earth to Stryxia. He picked something up along the way." And while I wasn't knowledgeable on every single species native to my planet, I had never seen the little dark red creature in the maintenance corridor before.

We hurried back inside. I engaged the controls to close the massive hull door, shutting us inside, hopefully not with whatever had destroyed the *sandspitter*. I gave a critical eye to the storage compartments and containers there. Nothing had been moved. Everything was locked in its place—no scratches, no claw marks, no strange smells, droppings, or anything to indicate something other than Rubi and I were in here. There were no signs of attempted destruction.

We returned to the control room. I locked the door behind us and went right to a terminal.

"Trakia Central, this is Rixen Alnas of cargo ship 39-A. Please respond."

There was nothing. Not even static or the sound of a relay transmitting. *Nothing.* I repeated my message, blood pressure rising in my two hearts.

"Don't tell me," Rubi said. "The communication link is down."

I rubbed my hand over my face. "It would appear so."

"One of those wires that creature chewed through?"

"No. Different area. There must be more damage farther back in the maintenance corridor that we were unable to see."

She sank into the seat next to mine and let out a sigh. I watched the emotions move over her beautiful features—worry, sadness, anxiety.

"I am sorry, Rubi," I said miserably. "This is going to take longer than planned."

She nodded, some of the color draining from her face. "I just don't want Andromeda to worry. Not right now when she's so close to having her baby. She has worried about me enough." Rubi shook her head. "Well, facts are what they are. What do we do now?"

"I am putting in an order for the computer to review the security footage of the cargo hold between the time we arrived and my closing of it. Maybe I can get an angle out the door to see what might have attacked the *sandspitter.*"

"How can I help?" she asked.

I nodded to the console next to me. "Let me change the language at your terminal," I said. "You can start looking up what that small creature is that we have living in the maintenance corridor by putting its description in the computer."

She nodded and waited as I reconfigured the interface to her native language.

We worked in quiet.

Looking through the footage provided by the computer, I saw nothing that stood out. The shifting shape of the small creature in the maintenance corridor wasn't in the cargo hold, and that space remained unchanged during the entire time we had been here. Also, cameras did not catch anything outside the opening, so the *sandspitter's* fate remained a mystery.

As for where the Rulgan operator had stopped, that was a different story. He'd made three stops, one of which was at a chaotic star base. I sat back, contemplating. He could have picked up any number of beings there, where security was nonexistent.

"What if whatever destroyed the *sandspitter* disguised itself and that's why we were unable to see it?" I mused.

"That would make it difficult to deal with," she said. "You mean it might be a chameleon?"

"A lizard?" That was all my translator gave me as a translation.

"No, I mean a being that can change its color to match its surroundings," she explained. "That's what chameleons do on Earth."

"It would explain why it has not shown up on any of the surveillance."

"On another topic," she said. "I think I have an idea of what is chewing those wires. Come take a look."

I rose and crossed to her terminal. The image on her screen was a creature with light red fur and a pair of horns. Its features were different, and the information about it showed a larger creature about double the size of what we saw.

"You think that's the creature in the maintenance corridor?"

"I think what we have here is a juvenile of this species." She tapped the screen. "I think what we have is a *frissa*. They are not affected by power surges like we are. In fact, they use them as shelter. They can be pests on ships, although not usually in this part of the galaxy."

I read over her shoulder, looking at the pictures as they scrolled by. The *frissa* was a nonaggressive being with a curiosity problem that caused it to wind up hitching rides on ships. "Is there any information on how to get them out of the guts of a ship?" I asked her.

"Well, it says here that they stay with their mothers until almost fully grown, so this one must've gotten separated from its parents somehow and I bet it's starving. They eat mostly *alugg* grubs, like this one." She pointed to the picture on the screen, showing a blobby thing the size of my foot, something we definitely did *not* have on Stryxia. "Any of these lying around the ship?"

"Sweet *Trall*, I hope not," I replied.

"That's what I thought," she said. "Which means

this creature is hungry and that might be why it's being destructive. Probably why it was afraid of you, too."

"So we have to wait until it starves to death?"

She swatted my arm. "No. We find something for it to eat and lure it out."

"I thought we established that we don't have any *alugg* grubs on board."

"No, but we have a food replicator. Maybe we can find out what the composition of the grubs are, you know, nutrient wise, and replicate something."

"I suppose that is quicker than waiting for it to starve."

She frowned at me. "More humane too. Come on, Rixen. These creatures aren't dangerous. This little one got lost. It's scared and hungry, not vicious."

"All right. We can try. You find out more about these *alugg* grubs and I will do a little more investigating on what our invisible visitor might be."

"It's a good plan," she said, but her smile was weary, and the color had faded from her cheeks.

"You know what? This can wait for a few minutes. You and I need something to eat and a little break too."

For once she didn't argue, but nodded. "I would like that."

I had the machine produce a variety of foods and spread them out on the floor of the control room. There was a perfectly fine common room, with tables and chairs for the crew, but staying in here for now, with a sealed door, gave some peace of mind until we knew what we were dealing with out there. She sat down beside me, legs curled to one side, and dug in.

We did not talk much as we ate. I was tired, too, and worried. But the break invigorated us both. By the time we were done, her eyes were bright again and she looked less tired.

We went back to work. I changed the parameters of the security system to pick up movement and potential life forms in different energy and light waves. And she managed to isolate the nutritional values of the *alugg* grubs and send those into the replicator.

"How do we make it look like a grub?" she asked, peering at the replicator screen.

"I think the best we are going to do is a tubular shape," I replied. "Maybe we can get the color right and the *frissa* will be so hungry it doesn't notice the difference."

"You've got to get the color. It looks kind of like a peach color."

"Peach? I don't have a definition for that."

"Right. Can't really describe colors on a translator. It's like this color." She plucked out a bracelet made up of many small beads. Her fingers closed around one. "This is peach. What is it called in Stryxian?"

"*Snone,*" I replied. "That color is called *snone.*" I caught her wrist and looked closely at the bracelet. She had several on her wrist that she wore all the time. "Where did you get this?"

Her eyes softened. "My son made it for me when he was in school. I've had to replace the elastic string many times, but the beads are all the same." Her fingers moved to the next bracelet over. "Andromeda made this one for me." It looked to be at least eight different-colored threads carefully knotted together, so the colors appeared in stripes. "And this one…" She shrugged one shoulder and ran her finger along a shiny silver chain dangling with charms. "I bought it for myself when I turned fifty. I just liked it."

I brought her wrist to my lips and kissed the pulse there. "They all suit you."

Her pulse fluttered beneath my mouth and she pulled in a quick, uneven breath. "So do you, damn you."

My lips curled into a grin. "You do not sound pleased about that."

"I'm not," she said, but her arm came to rest on my shoulder and her fingers played with the hair at the back of my head. "You're making my life complicated."

"You are doing the same to mine," I said. "Perhaps we are even."

"Really? I don't see you contemplating a move across the galaxy."

My chest contracted at hearing her say that she would consider a move to Stryxia. "Earth does not allow alien residents," I said. "Otherwise, I would."

I felt her body startle. "Seriously? You would move to Earth to be with me?"

"If we are meant to be, yes, I would. I would do anything to be with you." The words tumbled from my mouth. Even as her brow creased and her eyes widened. The hand on the back of my head went still. I pulled her arm away, kissed the back of her hand, and let it fall. "That's an *if*," I said.

Inside, I knew it wasn't an *if*, but she needed to hear that, to know that her fate was not already sealed. *It was*. Rubi Belta was mine. My female. My mate. But she was the one who would have to move across the galaxy to be with me, and that was no small thing. The fact that her daughter and grandchild lived here would likely help my cause, but it was by no means a done deal. Rubi would need to accept this and it might take time.

"Yes," she said. "If." She smoothed back her hair, something I rarely saw her do. Some of it had escaped its confines, sending tendrils around her face. "Okay." She closed her eyes, and opened them again. "One thing at a time. Let's get this grub to the *frissa*."

I had to take a pause to refocus my mind on the real issue at hand. "Yes," I said. "But we are not done talking about this."

"I know," she said. "I am very well aware."

"Good. And let me produce some of these...*peach* things for the *frissa* to eat. And hope it takes the bait."

"What are we going to do if it does eat this stuff?" she asked.

"I will tell the ship to adjust the sensor just outside the maintenance corridor. When it is tripped by this *frissa*, the lockdown door will drop and seal it out. That way it cannot do more damage."

"But what do we do with it then?"

"Feel free to add to this plan," I said. "Maybe if it is

no longer starving, your theory will be correct and it won't be so fierce."

"Perhaps then we can lure it to a room somewhere," she said. "When we get to Trakia, we'll figure out what to do with it." She made a face as an elongated blob plopped out of the replicator. "Ugh. I wouldn't eat that."

"Hopefully the *frissa* will." I picked up one tray and handed it to her.

"It smells bad, too."

Another fake grub came out of the machine. I picked up that one. "Let us go and get this over with," I said.

With the sensor linked to my earpiece, we left the control room and journeyed back through the corridors to the maintenance area. Just outside of it, Rubi put down her fake grub. I put the other one inside the opening, but not *all* the way in. The smell was very pungent.

"I hope the odor reaches the *frissa*," Rubi said, delicately placing a finger under her nose to block some of the smell.

"The entire ship is going to smell like this stuff," I said. "I fail to see how it could *not* smell this."

"Maybe it will scare away our other interloper," she said with a twist of her lips. "We should be so lucky."

"Come," I said. "We have done all we can do for now. We need some sleep. I am giving you the captain's quarters," I said with a smile. We went back through the halls and I stopped at a sliding door. "Here we are."

"Where are you sleeping?" she asked. "You must be exhausted."

I was. My days as a captain on a ship and all of the responsibilities that entailed, including little sleep, had ended many years ago. "I am fine. I will be in the control room if you need me."

"There are no other rooms?"

"There is a large open bunk room for when there is a full crew," I said. "But with only one operator on this trade run, the bunk room was used for storage. It's filled with overflow cargo." I gave her a stern look, just for fun. "There *was* a very large order of string lights from Earth."

"Hmm." Her eyes sparkled with humor. "Well, that settles it. You're coming to bed with me."

The statement shocked me into silence. I stood there, blinking down at her stunned into silence for a moment. "Pardon me?"

She waved her hand, almost as if annoyed. "I'm not inviting you to come in for *sex*," she said, and a cute flush warmed her cheeks. "I'm literally inviting you in to *sleep*. You need it. Those chairs in the control room are not comfortable for sitting, let alone sleeping."

I was still trying to grapple with her uttering the words, *you're coming to bed with me*. I couldn't deny I *had* dreamt of them. Under vastly different circumstances

When I still didn't say anything, she tsked. "Honestly, Rixen, even if we wanted to, neither of us has the energy for getting frisky right now."

"Oh, you're very wrong there," I said, ignoring the lack of energy part. I could muster some energy with proper motivation. "I very much want to. That is not a question."

Color bloomed brighter on her cheekbones. "Fine. I won't deny that I find you very attractive, and that there have been times when I've thought about what it would be like to—"

I placed a finger over her lips. "Do not say another word, or I will suddenly find a great deal of energy."

Her lips curved under my finger. "Very well. But I meant what I said." She pointed to the door. "Come in and get some sleep. If anything weird happens on the ship, the sensors will alert you, right?"

I nodded, looking at the door with something akin to dread. I wasn't sure how much sleep I would get lying next to her in the bed. While it was not small, there would be no way to lie there with her without touching. But there was no denying the pull, the acute yearning to just be near her. I rubbed my intensely burning eyes. "Very well, if you insist."

She laughed. "I do. I very much insist."

I opened the door. We both went in.

CHAPTER
Nine

Rubi

WE BOTH WENT IN.

The last time I'd been alone in a room with a man, it had been with the electrician, fixing a fried circuit breaker. Larry had been nice and he'd gotten the dishwasher running again; this was different.

Really different.

The stateroom was simple and utilitarian. There was the bed, some storage, and a room to the side, which I assumed was a bathroom. The lights were bright until Rixen flicked his fingers over a pad on the wall and dimmed them until they were very low. "Is that okay?" he asked. "I dare not turn them off completely in case my alerts go off while we're sleeping."

"It's fine," I said through a dry throat.

Rixen filled up the room with his presence. It was like a delicious cloud of masculinity. He was overwhelming to my senses. Part of me wanted to strip him down and find out if we had any energy in reserve, and part of me would be perfectly satisfied just staring at him for the next couple hours. He was beautiful. He always had been. Every time I'd gone into his shop had been a feast for the eyes.

And now we were alone in a small stateroom with a locked door. To sleep.

What was I thinking? How was I supposed to actually sleep in a bed with this guy?

But then again, the sight of a soft bed was very inviting. I sat on the edge, my tush sinking into the mattress, and the weariness came back like a tidal wave. I yanked off my boots, shrugged off my coat, and pulled back the covers.

Rixen was removing his shoes and the vest he wore, leaving him in his pants and a soft, snug-fitting shirt. It was an unspoken agreement that those were all the clothes we would be removing, to stay on the safe side. There was really no point in denying that our attraction was real, and very, very much on our minds.

The bed dipped as Rixen got in on the other side of it. I turned towards him just as he did the same. Our eyes locked. "This is very weird," I said.

Those sexy lips curled up at the edges. "It is." He reached out and tucked my hair behind my ear. "And also nice. I like seeing you in my bed."

I laughed. "Is this how you imagined it?"

"In one of my fantasies, yes."

"Do you have multiple?"

He raised a brow. "Don't you?"

"I suppose," I replied. "I take it the other ones are not as wholesome as this."

"You call this wholesome?" He let out a rusty chuckle. "Do you have any idea how hard my cock is right now?"

My eyes went wide. "It is not."

"It is," he replied without hesitation. "Would you like to see for yourself?"

I bit my bottom lip. "Don't tempt me."

A large hand slid up my arm, underneath the blanket. "I would like to do much more than tempt you, Rubi."

Oh, god, how was I supposed to sleep when my body was lighting up like a, well, like a Christmas tree? "We're supposed to be sleeping."

"And we will," he said. "But I was wondering something."

"What's that?"

"Would a kiss be asking too much?"

Yes. No. A kiss wasn't nearly enough. I wanted so much more. My body was coming alive for the first time in years. The last man I had kissed was my husband, before he left for war. But here I was, feeling… everything. "No," I said. "It's not too much to ask."

He shifted closer, but hesitated as if unsure if I had actually said yes, or he'd misinterpreted me.

I licked my upper lip. "Kiss me before I fall asleep, Rixen."

He closed the distance. His hand moved against the

center of my back, pulling me towards him. We were both still lying down. My hand went to his chest, where I could feel the muscles under his shirt. He had a wide, barrel chest. The scales, smooth when stroked in one direction, bristled against my hand when I touched in the other direction.

I had wanted to do this for a long time, to take my time and explore the way he felt, to touch those beautiful scales. It *was* one of the many things I had fantasized about. One of his wings stretched out and came around us. Again, it was a contrast. Tough and leathery on the outside, but soft and velvety on the inside. I longed to touch there, too.

"You can, you know." His dark gaze looked over me.

"I can what?"

In response, he lifted my hand and pressed it to the soft underside of his wing. "Touch me," he said raggedly. "Wherever you like. However you like."

I dragged in a breath as my fingers slid over the velvet there. "It's amazing," I murmured. My gaze flicked to his. "You're not going to let out any of those pheromones, are you? Because I really don't think I have the energy to—"

"No," he said. "My body doesn't have the energy, either." Then he seemed to think. "At least, I *hope* not. You know I have no control over it."

"I know that," I said. The downy inside of his wing rested on top of us like a warm, heavy blanket. "Did you say something about a kiss?" I asked.

"Demanding female." His fingers moved over my cheeks, my neck, slid over my shoulders. "I'm getting to that."

Then his lips were on mine, soft and gentle. Exploratory. My body felt like it was melting. An odd little noise came out of my mouth as my lips learned the shape and feel of his. It was like being woken up and dragged under the surface of water at the same time. If this was drowning, I never wanted to surface again.

"You taste incredible," he said, gently pulling back. "I knew you would."

"And you...you're..." I let out a groan. "I can't even talk."

He chuckled. "Then I must be doing something right."

"That's the problem. You do everything right."

"It doesn't have to be a problem," he said.

"I know," I said softly. "Let's just get out of here, okay? We can talk about...whatever this is between us when we're back in Trakia."

"Sensible," he grunted, and rolled back away from me. "I will admit that I feel very insensible at the moment."

"I know," I sighed, trying not to think about the state of his cock and how easy it would be to roll over to him and—

"If our trap works, I will be able to get into the maintenance corridor and repair the damage enough to get us back. You will be there for your grandchild's birth."

That wiped away the naughty thoughts trailing through my head. I nodded, but the truth was, we weren't sure about that. We really didn't know what we were up against aside from the little *frissa*, which might be the least of our issues.

"Hold me," I said in a rough voice. "Just don't let me go."

Lips brushed my forehead and my cheek, my lips. "Never."

We fell asleep like that, touching. Arms around each other and with his wing over both of us like an extra blanket. Sleep came fast and deep for me. Any doubt I had that I was exhausted faded away the instant my eyes closed. I didn't remember much after that until the bed jostled, dragging me out of sleep. "Wass going on?" I slurred as I sat up.

Rixen was up, pulling on his shoes. "All is fine," he said, but his voice was tense. "Stay here. I got an alert that our trap went off."

I got up, yanking on my boots. "I'm not missing this."

He made a face. "I knew you were going to say that."

I followed him out of the room. His hair was messed. His eyes still looked sleepy, as mine surely did too. I couldn't imagine the bags under them right now. Rixen grabbed our two blasters from the compartment by the control room and we hurried through the hallways. There was a noise, not a good one. A scrambling, scraping sound, and then something that sounded like the twisting of metal.

"*Trall*, what is going on?" he muttered.

I was half afraid to find out. There was a squeal, like something was afraid or in pain. We picked up our pace to keep moving.

We got to the place where we had left the fake grubs and there, as we'd hoped, the door was closed and the little *frissa* was huddled on our side of it. Only, it didn't appear to be alone.

And neither were we.

CHAPTER
Ten

Rixen

THE LITTLE *FRISSA* had curled itself into a small ball and was cowering in the corner. Its arms wrapped around its body. It let off pathetic little whimpering sounds as it tried to shrink away from something only it could see. The plates of fake grub were empty. It *had* fallen into our trap, but perhaps it had also fallen into another's trap, as the massive metal door, which now blocked off access to the maintenance corridor, had a huge dent in it that could not have been made by the small creature.

There were plenty of surprising beings in the galaxy. Species that possessed strength far beyond what one would think they should possess. The *frissa* was not one of them. I'd read the information we had on them. The only unusual trait they possessed was that of being unaffected by most forms of active raw energy, like electricity and the power that ran through the ship's system. Sure, too much of it would harm them, but they had a unique biology. That was why the little creature had sat in the nest of sparking wires. It was the *frissa's* only form of defense.

And we had taken it away.

"My god, Rixen," Rubi breathed. "Something tried to crash through that door."

"It wasn't the *frissa*," I said.

"I can see that," she said dryly. "What I *can't* see is whatever that *frissa* is afraid of."

"Why can't we?" I said in frustration, looking everywhere. I knew we weren't alone. I could feel a presence, like something was circling us, sizing us up. The air moved and held a strange smell.

"Oh!" Rubi jerked away from the sound of a growl directly behind her.

"Over here," I said, pulling her close. My gaze zeroed in on a scraping sound near one wall, then it shifted to the other. I felt a breeze as something moved past us quickly. "Arus would have some device that would allow us to see this being," I snarled.

"Rixen, that's it." Rubi's voice rose. "Our eyes can only see certain colors and light waves. It's possible there's another creature hiding in plain sight."

"What are you saying?"

"Maybe it's the lighting. Quick, can you turn off the light, or synch to the interface and change it through your earpiece?"

"Yes," I replied, touching my earpiece. I instructed

the ship's computer to lower the lights to ten percent. I had good dark vision, but I knew humans did not. I drew Rubi even closer and kept my arms around her so she wouldn't be afraid.

All the experience in the Morr-ta war had left an impact on me. While Rubi's husband had died, *I* had survived. I didn't thrive on fighting, like some of the warriors in my unit had. It had been a misery unmatched in any other part of my life. I even detested my memories of that time, so being in the midst of all this fear again, affected me. My wings shivered. I felt them release a pheromone—it was either aggression or something to calm. I didn't know which it would be.

"Your wings are doing that thing," said Rubi. "I smell almonds."

I didn't know what almonds were, but I felt relaxed —less tense and more alert. "They are trying to lower our stress," I said. "Not seduce you."

"I still feel stress," she muttered.

As the lights dimmed and my vision adjusted to it, I spied the softly glowing outline of...something. I wasn't sure what it was, but it was large and shifted around. We stood between it and the little, cowering *frissa*.

"I think I found our entity," I said. "To our left. Can you see it?"

"No," she said. "All I see is darkness. What does it look like?"

"A glowing outline, moving back and forth a little bit. Swaying." My vision was becoming clearer. The more my eyes adjusted to the darkness, the better I could see it. It was a hulking thing with long arms but no hands and rather flat, paddle-like appendages that waved at the ends. It had no eyes, but possessed a round, wide mouth that opened and closed rhythmically like breathing. It floated in the air.

"Any idea what it is?"

"No. But it backed away from us and seems to want the *frissa*."

"It destroyed the *sandspitter*, but it's after this little tiny creature?" It didn't make sense to me either. "It must want to eat it," she said.

I knew allowing the unknown being to attack the little *frissa* was not an option. It was completely helpless —because of us—and Rubi was looking at it like she was about to scoop it up and run off with it. "I will not shoot the other being," I said. "It has not attacked us."

She nodded. "If it's hungry, it's hungry. It doesn't deserve to be killed for that."

"But we need it to leave." The creature seemed to be reevaluating us. We'd startled it, but now it moved around with agitation. Those long limbs thrashed in frustration. "If it attacks," and I was beginning to think it would, "I'll have to shoot."

Rubi looked down at the little *frissa.* "What is it about this little guy that is so tasty?"

I thought about the *sandspitter* and the mess of raw electricity sparking in the maintenance corridor. "Energy."

"What?"

"It feeds on energy. The *frissa's* body must hold a certain frequency, like the *sandspitter's* energy cell, which it tore the *sandspitter* apart to get to. This little *frissa* must be a delicacy to this creature."

"Well, I'm sorry, but I won't let it feed off this little guy." Rubi edged away from me and toward the cowering little *frissa.* "There are other ways of getting energy. I wish we had another *sandspitter* to feed to it."

We didn't have another vehicle with those power cells, but we did have something else. I barked out a laugh. "Arus is going to be upset."

Rubi shot me a vexed look. "Want to fill me in?"

"I have a shipment of Gamorian converter cells in the cargo hold. The energy signature is very similar. They would be a feast for this being." The being in question was growing steadily impatient. It flicked out an arm. One of the paddle-shaped appendages brushed my shoulder, sending painful jolts through my body. "*Trall*," I snarled.

Rubi yelped. "Are you okay? Did it hurt you?"

"It puts out a zap," I said. "Give me your blaster and try to grab that *frissa*, if it doesn't bite you."

She didn't hesitate. She gave me her weapon and freed up both arms to reach for the small creature. This time, it kept its teeth tucked away and leapt willingly into Rubi's embrace. She held the small *frissa* close. "It's okay, little one," she soothed. "We'll get you out of here."

I hoped so. It had certainly enraged the hunter to see its prey scooped up and harder to get to. I also sensed that it didn't want to harm us. "Move toward the passageway," I said to Rubi. "We can use the *frissa* to lure this entity to the cargo hold where I can give it the cells. Perhaps that will satiate its hunger."

"If it doesn't attack you again."

"It could have taken us out by now," I said. "Look what it did to the door and the *sandspitter*. Yet it has not attacked us."

Sweat shined on Rubi's forehead. Her mouth was a tight line, but she held the whimpering *frissa* like a baby, protecting it. "'Yet' is the important word here, and it *did* strike out at you, so be careful."

I looked at her, fiercely. "I will. You are holding the *frissa* that this being wants to eat. If it wants to live, it will not come near you."

She shook her head, but together, we moved toward the hallway that would lead us to the cargo hold. The entity, as I'd hoped, followed.

"Run," I said to Rubi, as we passed into the hallway and the lights became brighter. I could no longer see it or tell how close it was, but with a little *frissa* with us, I knew it was following close on our heels.

I was very curious what this was. Somewhere, it had to be listed in some database. It certainly wasn't a native species of Stryxia. I would feel sorry for it if my shoulder wasn't still burning from its stinging touch.

"This way," I said to Rubi, taking a right turn and swinging an arm around her to keep her close. The last thing I wanted was for her to fall behind with the hungry creature in pursuit. She was a little out of breath. The *frissa* was the size of a solid baby. It was hard to run with one of them. But I could not take her burden from her, as I now held both blasters, and I needed to be prepared to use them.

At last, we turned the final corner and entered the large, well-lit space at the cargo hold. Containers filled the space, both big and small, with pathways between them. I tapped my earpiece. "Computer, tell me where I can find the shipment of Gamorian converter cells."

A mechanical voice replied in my ear, "A container of twelve Gamorian converter cells is located in row D, location 3-B4."

I bit back a curse. It was, of course, on the other side of the cargo bay. I could feel the air around us moving; the creature was incensed we had run off with the *frissa*.

"It is on the far side," I said, leading Rubi through the aisles and towards the location of Arus' Gamorian converter cells. He would just have to wait for another shipment. And despite the ordeal we were going through, I would still get an earful about him not getting them.

As we ran, I caught glimpses of a spark spraying here, a scrape there, as the invisible creature followed us through the cargo hold. It was close. The scales on the back of my neck stood up as the proximity of its electrical current played against my skin.

"There!" I pointed to a nondescript container that came up to my knees. According to the coordinates I had received from the computer, that was it. I ran up to it, holding my blasters in the general direction that I sensed the being was in. I tucked one into my belt as I pressed my hand against the container's panel. Thank goodness my palm print would open it. With a hiss, the lid unsealed and it lifted a small amount. I pulled it all the way open. Inside were rows of converter cells, glowing a gentle green in their padded case.

"Is this what you want?" I pulled one out and held it out. "All the energy you could want. If you can leave us alone now."

I had no idea if this being could understand what I was saying. I spoke in Stryxian. Rubi's translator converted it to a language she understood, but this creature had no such device that I knew of. I slowly stooped down and rolled the cylinder along the floor, towards the creature.

I stood up, hands outstretched. "You can have it all," I said. "No one needs to get hurt."

The cylinder on the floor was still for a moment, then, suddenly, glass burst and the green solution inside appeared to be sucked straight out of it and disappeared.

I pointed to the rest. There were eleven more canisters. That was a lot of energy. It was a huge order from Arus, which I would have to reorder and not charge him for, of course. A small price to pay to satiate this creature's hunger and keep us safe.

I looked over my shoulder. "Take the *frissa* back to the control room and shut the door," I said. "I will return soon."

Eyes wide, she shook her head. "I can't leave you."

I sighed, touched that she did not want to leave me, but this *needed* to happen. I needed to get her and the *frissa* away from this being. Another of the cylinders inside the case cracked open. The contents disappeared.

"Please, Rubi. Just this once, do as I say."

She pursed her lips and her face crumpled. Tears filled her eyes. She held the little creature, which was still and quiet in her arms, and stepped away.

"Go," I said. "I love you, Rubi. Trust me."

She spun away and hurried down the aisle towards the corridor that would take her to the control room, but not before I saw the tears fall. I frowned with worry. I had made her cry, but I wasn't sure what I had said that caused it.

Meanwhile, the being, which was invisible in the bright lights of the cargo hold, was working through each canister, one by one. When the last one had been cracked and consumed, I touched my earpiece. "Computer, open the main hull door."

The massive cargo bay door cracked open on its massive hinges and slowly continued to open. Now that Rubi was out of here, I ordered the computer to turn the lights off in the cargo hold.

It went dark, except for the glowing being. It glowed brightly, now with a rainbow of colors. I pointed towards the opening. "Go," I said, gesturing towards the outside, hoping it would understand what I meant. It looked vibrant, healthy, and outstandingly beautiful as it hovered there, arms, limbs, undulating like waves. Its mouth still opened and closed, but it was backing away, moving towards the opening. It pressed its paddle-like appendages together in front of its face, and made a bowing motion.

Stunned, I mirrored it, placing my palms together and lowering my head just enough to let it know I acknowledged the gesture.

Then, it was gone. It turned into a flow of light and poured out of the large bay door.

I jogged over to the opening and looked out to see a spear of light shoot up into the dark, early morning sky and disappear. Clouds, heavy and thick, hung low and ominous in the sky.

I sagged against the massive entryway and ran my fingers through my hair. One problem down. Now I had repairs to do. "Computer, close the main hull door."

It closed as I walked through the cargo hold to the control room. The moment I opened the door, Rubi threw herself into my arms. I gathered her close, breathing in her scent and feeling her warm softness close around me like the most wonderful blanket I had ever known.

"Is it gone?" Her voice was muffled by my chest.

"Yes. It consumed the energy and shot up into the sky." I ran a hand over her soft hair. "I think that's all it wanted—enough energy to be able to leave, and maybe return home."

She leaned back and looked up at me, eyes bleary with spent tears. "Can *we* go home soon?"

I thought about the swirling, angry-looking clouds

and winced. "I need to do the repairs in the maintenance corridor," I said. "And I'm concerned that we are about to have a storm."

"A storm? I've never been here when there's been any sort of weather."

"It does happen this time of year, occasionally. We experience them now that the domes are down and the atmosphere is rebuilding. The Sanrous Plains are vulnerable to them. Let me check." I went to a terminal and did a scan of the environment around the ship. Sure enough, it returned with the high probability of a storm.

I sighed. "I will work as quickly as I can," I said to Rubi. "But I cannot promise that we will be able to leave before the storm hits. If we can't, we may be stuck here a few more days."

Her mouth dipped at the edges, but she nodded. "As long as I can get word to Andromeda that I am okay and hear that *she* is doing well, it's fine."

She would likely miss the birth of her grandchild, and the humans in Trakia would probably not get their Christmas orders before the holiday, but we had survived, and the little *frissa* curled up sound asleep on Rubi's chair could rest easy knowing that it was no longer being hunted.

"I made it another one of those fake grubs," she said. "I had to do something while I was waiting, not knowing if you were dead or not." She cast me a dark look. "Don't do that again. I can't handle another male I love leaving for possible death." She shook her head. "I don't have it in me."

I cupped her face in my hands, understanding, now, why she had cried. "You will never have to worry about that again. I will never leave you."

She tilted her head up and went up on her toes as my mouth came down on hers. It was a long, deep kiss of bonding and promise and love. "I will never leave you either," she said.

"Those are the most wonderful words anyone has ever spoken to me," I said.

"Well, they're true," she said. "Now, let's go fix this ship."

CHAPTER
Eleven

Rubi

THE LITTLE *FRISSA* was not letting me out of his sight. He *was* a he, as a peek under the hood made clear. He'd scarfed down another fake grub while Rixen had been getting the mystery creature out of the cargo hold. Cooking and feeding people had always soothed me when I was nervous, and the replicator was the closest thing I had to a kitchen, and the *frissa* was the only thing to feed. He'd been eager to eat, too, and afterward had settled down for a sleep.

I picked him up and carried him with me as Rixen and I went back down to the maintenance corridor, a place I was *really* looking forward to never seeing again. He carried a large case of tools to repair the damage that this little creature had done. My chest was lighter with so much less worry. Now, the only thing on my mind was getting a message to Andromeda, who was undoubtedly worrying by now, *or* thinking I'd eloped with Rixen.

The first thing he was concentrating on was the communication system, so we could message Trakia about what had happened and ask them about the incoming storms. They did not look good. A glance out of any window revealed a mess of dark blue clouds and winds that pushed the grasses on the Sanrous Plains flat against the ground.

"This ship can handle space but can't fly through a storm?" I asked, hoping against hope that we would be able to get out of here, at least by flying through it.

"These ships are engineered and built for the weightlessness of space," he said. "It actually takes quite a bit of power for them to leave the ground. High winds, snow, and ice could cause us to crash."

"Wait, you said snow?"

He waved a hand as he reconnected two tubes that had been leaking fluid. "It is rare, but it happens. And according to the sensors, snow is likely to fall with this storm."

"Well," I said, with a shake with my head. "I wasn't expecting a white Christmas."

"What do you mean?" He looked up from where he had been buried in a nest of circuits and wires. There was a smudge of grease on his cheek and his hair was mussed. He looked unbearably sexy.

"It's an Earth thing," I said. "A white Christmas just means we have fresh snow on Christmas. It's a treat.

Very festive. Not all parts of Earth even get snow, but it's a thing."

He grunted and went back to his work. "Snow on Stryxia is no small matter," he said. "Storms are brutal and last for days, grounding all vessels coming or going."

I couldn't help but smile. It had the potential to be a romantic thing, if we weren't trapped here.

"There's nothing to smile about," he said. "We may not be leaving this spot until the storm passes. By then, your grandchild will have been born."

I petted the slumbering bundle in my lap, which let out a sleepy snort. "I've come to peace with that," I said. "As long as the baby is born healthy and her mom is safe, that's all that matters. I'll catch up with my grandbaby later. We'll have plenty of time, now that I'm staying on this planet."

I was rewarded with a blinding smile. "I love hearing you say that. That you are staying."

"Well, I can't very well leave now, can I?" I raised one brow. "It's not every day that a fifty-something-year-old woman falls in love again. I know a good thing when I see it."

"So do I," he said. "I knew you were a good thing when I first laid eyes on you."

"You know," I said. "*If* we're stuck here for a couple days, I know how we can pass the time."

He looked at me warily. "Snuggling with that creature on your lap?"

"No," I said. "But it would involve something in *your* lap."

His eyes widened and the tool fell from his hand. "I thought you said we would talk about this when we returned to Trakia."

I shrugged one shoulder. "Maybe I changed my mind. Maybe I know what I want *now*, and I don't see a reason to wait. You are mine, Rixen." I sent him a wicked grin with a mind full of dirty thoughts. "And I *really* want to see you naked."

He closed his eyes. "You absolutely cannot say those things if you want me to finish these repairs."

I crossed my legs and petted the little *frissa* in my lap. "Well, hurry up, then," I said sweetly. "Don't keep either of us waiting."

CHAPTER
Twelve

Rixen

I HAD LEARNED many things during my time with Rubi. One of them being how difficult it is to concentrate with a beautiful female nearby. Especially one that is yours, who desires you, and who wants to make love to you when you're done with a task.

This task was made harder by the knowledge that Rubi wanted me. She sat nearby as I worked on the communication panel, deep in the maintenance corridor. The *frissa* had done a number on this area. Apparently he had thought this small sector was a good place to hide from the *nimm*—that was the name of the species that had been pursuing our little *frissa*. As I worked to replace broken parts and reconnect pulled-out interfaces, Rubi chatted away.

I loved the sound of her voice. She could make herself laugh, and did so often. I loved the twinkle in her eye and the way she looked at me as if she had secret, special thoughts she wanted to share with me.

I had a feeling the *frissa* would be staying with us. Rubi had settled him peacefully on her chair in the control room and we'd left him there to go work on the damage in this part of the ship. Rubi was pondering names for the small creature, which was enamored with her—*as was I*. The *frissa's* home planet was very far away from here, and there had been no talk about returning him, where he'd be ill-equipped to live in a wild place, so it seemed we had a pet. Aside from having to feed him foul-smelling fake grubs, he was a pleasant enough little creature. He seemed devoted to Rubi, as if he had chosen her as his new mother.

With the last two interface tubes reconnected and the gel conduits reestablished, I unfolded from my cramped spot at the end of the corridor and stretched. "That should be it," I said. "Let us see if we can contact Trakia."

Rubi's eyes lit up. "Yes. Let's go back to the control room. Can I help you carry anything?"

I smiled. "No," I said. "I have it in hand. The stabilizers will be another job and they are in worse condition than I thought. I am thinking we should ask Trakia to send a transport out to collect us once the storm is over," I said. "It will get us home faster and a more qualified repair technician can fix this ship."

Rubi nodded. "The faster the better," she said. "As cozy as it is here, I miss my family."

"Andromeda will be very happy to get you back,

I'm sure." I held her hand with my free one. "You are fortunate to have a good relationship with your daughter."

"We had only each other for a long time," she said.

We walked back through the ship to the control room. The *frissa* was still curled in a ball, sleeping away. The little creature snored occasionally, which I had to admit, was very cute. Rubi lightly petted the little creature without waking him up. "I hope he gets along with Haggis," she said.

"Haggis gets along with everyone," I replied as I booted up the communication system from default. "It will be good for him to have a new friend."

"That's true," she said. "And the baby will have several pets looking after her."

"Her?" I asked. "I thought Andromeda and Xarik had chosen to not learn the gender of their child."

She just shrugged. "I have a sense about these things. Xarik may not have used his powers to learn the gender, but my gut tells me it's going to be a girl." Her smile faltered. "Who is being born today, if those estimates are correct."

"Not an estimate," I said as the system lit up on the screen. "Stryxian medics know the exact day and time a birth will happen. I am very sorry you will miss it."

A crackling sound came through the system. "This is Trakia Central Control," said the voice of a communications officer. "Go ahead."

I had never felt such relief at hearing a voice on the other end of the coms. "Trakia Central, this is Rixen

Alnas of cargo ship 39-A. I have Rubi Belta and one other life form on board. Our vessel is disabled on the Sanrous Plains and a storm is approaching. We are requesting transport to Trakia village."

"We are glad to hear from you, Rix," said the operator. "The commanders have been worried about you, but we have been unable to send out probes or scouts due to the storm."

"It's affecting the village?"

"It has stopped all travel for the last day. It is on track to hit the Sanrous Plains imminently."

"I know. The ship's environmental scanners indicate the storm is about to hit us here. I was hoping to beat it out of here, but that seems impossible."

"It is, Rix," replied the officer. "However, we *will* get a transport out the moment weather clears here. Do you have adequate life support and supplies?"

"Yes," I said. I gave him a rundown of the status of the ship, leaving the drama of the *nimm* and the *frissa* for a later day, when we arrived at home on Trakia. "Rubi Belta would very much like to have contact with her daughter, Andromeda, who is scheduled to deliver her first child today."

"Affirmative, Rix. Let me patch you in to her com."

Rubi perked up and moved to stand beside me. There was a pause on the com. Her hand closed over my shoulder. "I hope she's okay," she murmured.

"Xarik will make sure she is, I promise you that," I said.

There was another spit of static, then a smooth, female voice came on the line. "Mom?"

The hand on my shoulder squeezed. "Andromeda? How are you? Are you okay?"

There was a pause. "Yes, I'm fine. Where *are* you?"

"I'm out on the Sanrous Plains with Rixen still," she replied. "It's a long story. I'll tell you about it when we get back. Do we have a baby yet?"

"No baby yet," Andromeda replied. "But soon. Contractions have started, but I'm in between them right now. I'm at the medic and everything is going smoothly. They have me hooked up to some machine that monitors everything and blocks most of the pain. Xarik's here, but he won't stop pacing."

I felt Rubi relax. Her hand, which had been gripping increasingly tighter, eased a fraction. "You're going to be just fine, honey. I love you and can't wait to see you."

"I love you, too, Mom." A little bit of nerves seeped into Andromeda's voice. "We're having a storm here, so they'll let us know when you can come back?"

"Absolutely. I'll be there as soon as I can. I can't wait to meet my new grandbaby."

"And then we have two weeks before you have to go back to Earth," she said. "That'll be good. Maybe you can extend it a few more days. And then you have another trip scheduled to come out in six months, right?"

Rubi turned her gaze to mine. Joy twinkled in her dark blue depths. "Oh, honey," she said without unlocking her eyes from mine. "Plans have changed."

"Oh my god, did you get it on with Rix?" came the excited question from Andromeda.

"He's sitting right here," said Rubi, warningly. "And let's just say, I think I'll be staying a lot longer than two weeks."

"No way. I knew it." I heard her voice muffle as she presumably turned to Xarik. "My mom and Rix. I told you, didn't I?"

Xarik's response wasn't audible, and that was probably a good thing. The male was likely not interested in my bonding at that moment, with his mate in active labor.

"Andromeda, I have a lot to fill you in on," she said. "But right now, you just put your worries away and concentrate on bringing that baby into the world, okay? And merry Christmas, if I don't get back in time."

"Merry Christmas, Mom. And Rix." Andromeda had to go after that. Her contractions were starting up again and now that communication with Trakia had been established and our location marked, there was nothing we could do but wait. I had a female to get better acquainted with.

I swiveled in my chair and gazed up at her. "What would you like to do now, Ms. Belta?"

"Ms. Belta, eh?" Her eyes heated. "I don't know, Mr. Alnas. I'm not feeling tired, are you?"

I shook my head. "Feeling very much awake."

"And I'm not hungry. For food."

"No. Me neither."

Her glance slid to the *frissa*. "He's not waking up anytime soon."

I rose from my chair, standing close to her, looming a little bit, but I couldn't help it. I wanted her with a ferocity that was almost overwhelming. "Then maybe we can step into the stateroom." I gestured towards the window, where thick snow had begun to fall. "We have nothing else to do for a while."

She raised her hand, placed it on the center of my chest and slowly slid it down, over my belly. Her fingers hooked in the waist of my pants, making my breath shudder. "I think we can find some things to do to pass the time, don't you?" she asked silkily.

My restraint snapped like a twig. A feral growl slipped through my lips as I scooped her up into my arms.

She let out a small squeal and roped her arms around my neck. "That sounds like a yes," she said as I strode through the control room and into the small stateroom and placed her on her feet.

It was like something out of a dream. "Do you want this?" I asked her. "Be sure, because there is no taking it back. When I take you in that bed, you will be mine."

She sighed and rested her head against my shoulder. "Rixen, I've been yours for a long time. Take me. Make love to me. I *am* yours."

CHAPTER
Thirteen

Rubi

I WAS FILLED with anticipation as our eyes met in the dimly lit room. My heart raced uncontrollably in my chest as I watched Rixen slowly pull off his boots.

I couldn't help but admire his rugged charm. He was an alpha male through and through, but there was so much warmth beneath that gruff exterior. As I approached him, our gazes locked once more—a silent promise passed between us, which sent shivers down my spine.

Rixen broke into a warm smile. "Are you sure about this?" he asked again.

"Oh, yes," I replied. "More than ready."

He held out his hand invitingly before pulling me in closer, and I allowed myself to be pulled into his embrace willingly—his aura wrapping around me like silk. He was like a private haven amidst the crazy things we'd gone through on this ship. The world outside melted away as time seemed to stand still within the cocoon of our chemistry—an undeniable passion only known by those who dared to open their hearts, no matter how scary it was.

I slid my arms up and over Rixen's broad shoulders while his gentle fingers journeyed along the curves of my back, drawing patterns that traced the lines of my own desire beneath the single layer of fabric separating us.

His mouth lingered an inch away. His eyes, which weren't quite so black anymore, moved over my face. "You are mine, Rubi. My mate. Your employment on Earth has ended," he declared. "You will stay with me, here, on Stryxia."

I already knew this. In my gut, I knew after that first kiss that I wasn't going back—not permanently, anyway. My future was here, with him, with my daughter and her family. I wouldn't be honoring the ones I lost by refusing to embrace this amazing chance at love. It wasn't what my husband and son would have wanted for me. I ran my fingers through his hair. "Do you know anyone who can arrange transport of some of my things on Earth?" I asked with a grin. "Or should I ask around?"

His smile was breathtaking. "Cheeky female." He gently smacked my ass, making me chuckle. "Anything you want, I will grant you. Say that you will stay with me."

"I can't give you up, Rixen," I said. "I'm yours as

much as you're mine."

I could feel his relief as he saw the truth of my words in my eyes. "My mate," he said again. "I never thought I would say those words."

Inevitability took hold and our bodies drew towards one another like a force written in stars centuries ago, destined solely for our bonding.

Our kiss started tenderly—a featherlight touch igniting sparks deep within, as if exploring territories previously uncharted, yet somehow familiar at once. This was no ordinary touch. It was an electrifying connection of one mate recognizing the other. Rixen's fingertips danced along my spine, coaxing me closer as our lips melded together in a tantalizing dance, like music played only for us, long-lost melodies spoken through the language of love.

Time slipped away, meaningless. Our mouths parted momentarily, gasps for air blended with the occasional adjustment of bodies. I felt like a teenager discovering passion anew. It was intoxicating, exciting.

Breathless and hungry once more, our lips pulled together again. Years melted away. Clothes became burdensome barriers briefly acknowledged before we clumsily worked them off. My shirt went flying across the room. A boot hit the wall.

Reality—*what was that*? We were someplace very far from reality, and I could let myself indulge in it because staying on Stryxia meant this was my reality. My soul was intertwined with this male whose black eyes now held a touch of blue. This was a bond that went beyond the physical, but tethered our hearts into unity. His sizzling touches ignited flames that would never be extinguished. With time, they'd only grow.

As we waited for our rescue, and the storm raged outside, he nudged me down, onto the bed, and lay down beside me. My heart thumped loudly in my chest. This was it—the moment I had been waiting for. The moment when everything would change. I took a deep breath and listened to the dull roar of the snow and ice outside, barely louder than the sound of our uneven breaths. The window revealed a white blur. But what captivated me most was not the storm, but the male leaning over me.

He gazed down at me, dark eyes alight with pleasure and love. My heart fluttered at that familiar sight and I felt myself falling deeper into him.

"Rubi," he said softly, running a possessive hand up my now bare body. His weight rested on one side as he lay beside me. One hand held his head while the other moved over me, skimming over my legs, belly, breasts.

"Hi," I replied with a nervous smile. He was seeing me naked for the first time, but he didn't seem disappointed by what lay underneath my clothes. His gaze was almost reverent.

"You are perfect."

I let out a weird-sounding laugh. "Hardly."

He reached for my hand, twined his fingers through mine, and kissed my knuckles. "Do you doubt the words of your mate?"

I rolled my eyes. "No, but I'm aware that I don't look like I did in my twenties."

His gaze locked with mine. "You belonged to another, then. Now, you are mine. My *mala* knew that you were my mate the moment I saw you. The connection we shared the day we first saw each other was real. You took my breath away. You still do. And now…" He looked me over like someone surveying the most delicious meal they'd ever seen. "I no longer have to imagine what being with you would be like. I can savor every inch of you." His mouth dipped, pulling one hardened nipple into his mouth and making me gasp. "I will make you scream my name, Rubi."

Right there and then, the traces of worry about my body evaporated. Rixen's desire was real and any issues were, well, *mine,* and I had no use for them here. I arched my back and just let myself feel.

His touch sent delicious shivers throughout my body as everything that we'd gone through over the last few days flashed through my mind like snapshots from an old movie reel—moments of laughter, terror, excitement—to these moments shared only between us two. I knew once we were back in Trakia, we'd be that older couple who couldn't keep their hands off each other in public places. Being with him was simply intoxicating and it had nothing to do with the pheromones his wings were releasing, filling the air between us with a scent that reminded me of jasmine.

But tonight…tonight would always be different than any other night after. Tonight marked a special milestone in our relationship: formalizing our bond as mates —such a strange, yet appropriate term for what we were becoming. His lips met mine gently but urgently. My fingers instinctively ran over his scales, through his hair, pulling him closer to me with every second that passed. Our bodies pressed against each other as if we were finally able to become one after waiting for this moment. His touch on my skin set me on fire, igniting uncontrolled desire deep within and causing an inferno I could not, and did not want to, control anymore.

We melted into each other's embrace like two pieces of a puzzle fitting perfectly together. His body shifted to hover above me. His heavy cock rested on my belly as his mouth laved my breasts and feasted on my skin. He explored every inch of my body with his hands and lips, eliciting moans and gasps from me in response.

But amidst all the passion and heat between us, there was a tenderness that couldn't be ignored. It radiated from him in waves as he held my face in his hands while kissing away any doubt I might have had left.

"Your cunt is wet," he rasped against my neck. "Are you ready for me, Rubi?"

Oh god, no one had *ever* talked to me like that, and it was shockingly hot coming from Rixen. There wasn't even a whisper of disrespect, but rather, he sounded reverent.

I closed my eyes. He was big and I hadn't been with a man in a long time. "Yes," I said, hoping it was true. "It's, um, been a while, so…" I couldn't finish that sentence.

He could sense my hesitation. A warm hand moved over my cheek. "I will be gentle with you." He spread my legs wide and moved between them. The head of his cock pressed to my sex and penetrated. Instead of pain, my body welcomed him. He slid inside, stretching me, filling me. "Are you okay?"

Oh, I had to talk? An impossible task, considering how incredible I felt. How alive I felt. "Yeah," I got out, somehow. "Hmm. Good."

As our bodies moved together rhythmically, becoming attuned to each other's desires, I let myself go completely, giving in to the sensations fully, without any fear or reservation. His muscles bunched as he moved, thrusting in time to my own movements.

He whispered words of love and sometimes uttering Stryxian words my translator couldn't decipher for me, but I knew what he was saying. They were things that didn't always have words. Feelings that defied language.

My body coiled like a spring, tight with desire. I felt it build like a wave rising inside me, and let out a cry as it crashed. His wings blacked out all the light as they covered us like a tent. My senses filled with the scent of his pheromones, increasing everything. Making my body feel like it was coming apart. Heat spiraled through me, lighting up every inch of skin as my orgasm pulsed and throbbed.

He thrust harder, faster, then found his own shuddering release with a groan.

"Oh," I said breathlessly. "Oh my."

"Female," he grunted, sliding out of me and over to my side. "I had no idea. Will it always be like that?"

The awe in his voice was adorable. I rolled toward him and pressed a kiss to his mouth. "With us? Probably. We're bonded mates after all." I meant to make that sound cheeky, to diffuse the intensity of the moment, but if there was ever an appropriate moment for intensity, this was it. "Your eyes, Rixen…" I ran my fingertips over his brows. "They're dark blue. Like mine."

He gathered me in his arms. "I know. I felt them change."

"Did it hurt?"

"On the contrary, they finally *stopped* hurting," he said. "That's how I knew."

We held onto each other tightly, not wanting this moment to end but knowing deep inside that it was only the beginning. As we lay there, basking in the afterglow, I couldn't help but think how incredibly lucky I was to have found such a soulmate. Rixen completed me in every possible way. I'd never thought I'd have another chance at this kind of love.

We stayed there, entwined together under a blanket as the storm raged, losing track of time and talking about anything and everything. My heart swelled with so much emotion, I thought it might burst. And as we drifted off into a peaceful sleep in each other's arms, I knew that this love—*our love*—was something we'd cherish forever. We were truly bound together on this, the strangest Christmas Eve I'd ever known in my life.

Epilogue

"ALL OF THEM? You fed *all* of them to a *nimm*?"

"I sighed, amazed by how closely Arus' reaction to losing his order of Gamorian converter cells adhered to how I'd envisioned it. "To save our lives, yes."

"To save a *frissa*," he said with a scowl.

"Rubi's *frissa*," I corrected. "And possibly us, if we had angered it enough. You saw what it did to the sand-spitter."

We stood at the counter in my shop. It wasn't even open. Rubi and I had arrived in Trakia only hours ago. After being picked up by a transport when the storm had subsided, Rubi and I had gone directly to the medic to find Andromeda and Xarik gazing at their baby in pure awe. The baby had arrived—a girl, as Rubi had predicted. She had the smooth, scaleless skin of her mother and the wings of her father, and was perfect as we watched her sleep in her mother's arms. They had named her Emi, a favored female name in Stryxian, and also one that was used on Earth.

Rubi had gazed at the new family with so much love in her eyes that my heart had squeezed. Then, she turned to me with that same look and I could have fallen apart on the spot. So great was the love this female had for those lucky enough to be in her life. My mala had blessed me with the finest mate a male could have.

I was Rubi's mate, but I'd wanted to give them a little time on their own, so I'd left the four of them, to stop in at my shop and make sure I had received no important messages. Snow had fallen thick and deep in Trakia, covering the buildings with a white mantle and making everything glisten. I could hear the beautiful tinkling voices of children—not many, but there were more on the way, adding to our growing, blended population of human-Stryxians. The walkways were clear when Arus had burst in, having heard a "rumor" that his Gamorian converter cells had been lost. He was *not* pleased.

"You would have done the same for your mate," I told him, knowing it was true. He would move the ground itself to please Keira.

He harrumphed. "I am glad you and Rubi are safe," he said grudgingly.

"Why, *thank* you," I said with a helping of sarcasm, although I took no offense. Arus had bluster, but he was the first one to look out for others and offer help. "It is a pleasure having customers who care for the wellbeing of others."

Arus rolled his eyes. "Of course, I care, Rix. I just also care about the Gamorian converter cells I ordered. You put in for another set to arrive soon?"

"Doing it as we speak," I said. "No additional expense to you."

"Good." He nodded. "I got you the trees you wanted."

"The what?" I looked up from the console. "I ordered trees?"

"Yes, you wanted trees that resembled those on Earth that the females wanted," he said impatiently. "Remember? You had me get more from my supplier in the northern sector."

"Ah, yes." I completed Arus' order and, seeing no pressing matters in my messages that couldn't wait, I closed out the screen and looked up at him. "Thank you. Unfortunately, the holiday has passed."

Arus smacked me on the arm. "The trees arrived before you did, and all the humans decided to delay the holiday celebration by a day so you two could be here to enjoy it."

"They did?"

"Yes, and since these holidays are new to us, no Stryxian objected. We are simply bemused by their customs." He shrugged. "So I suspect that as we speak, your ship is being unloaded and cargo dispersed."

My eyes widened at the thought of a free-for-all on my ship.

Arus waved a hand, seeing my worry. "There is a manifest and it is being respected. Our friend Mazak is overseeing it all. Everyone is getting what they ordered." He cast me a dark look. "Except for me."

I laughed, relieved that my ship was in good hands with the ex-bounty hunter cyborg who had taken up farming in his retirement from his former dangerous profession. "You will get your Gamorian converter cells," I said. "Consider this a lesson in patience."

"It is a lesson, all right," he said. "In finding another merchant to supply my power needs."

I raised one eyebrow. "I am the only one willing to track down your strange, and often volatile, orders, Arus."

"I know it." He grunted and gestured for the door. "Come on, Rix. If you are done in here, let us go get something to drink. We have your new bonding to celebrate."

As much as I yearned to be back with Rubi, I nodded and followed him out. On the walk outside of my shop, I stopped in my tracks and looked around. "What is going on?"

Arus stood beside me. "They are decorating."

Everywhere I looked, Stryxians and humans were hanging those string lights up on homes. Candles were lit in windows. Ropes of glittering stuff called "garland" was being strung up, and the trees I had Arus bring from the north were visible in windows and were also getting lit up with those strings of colorful lights. "I hear singing."

"I know," he said, sounding bewildered. "They have these songs they apparently sing this time of year. Even Keira is singing, but—I love that female to my bones— she should not really sing." He dropped his voice for that bit. "Do not tell her I said that."

"I would not." I looked around at the happy faces. Some carried colorfully wrapped gifts. A Stryxian male and his offspring were making a figure from the snow while his human mate laughed and helped. "This is amazing."

"It is," he said. "I have a feeling it is going to be this way every year at this time. It will certainly keep you in business."

"Then I will have no need to fill your impossible orders," I muttered, but the joke was light and I meant no malice. It was impossible to feel anything but plea- sure at the scene before me.

A hand slid up my arm. "There you are."

The smooth, welcome voice had me smiling before I even looked down to see Rubi beside me. She was beaming. "See? The string lights are totally worth it."

"They are very colorful," I said, turning to her. "How was your visit with Andromeda?"

"She is very pleased for us, and both she and Xarik would like to welcome you to the family more formally when they're home with the little one." Rubi smiled up at me. "She is so very happy that Emi will have a grandfather."

Rubi's words were like a shock. "*Grandfather?*"

She laughed. "What else would you be? You may

not be Andromeda's father, but you are my partner, and that means you'll be part of the baby's life. You will be important to her."

Everything around us faded into a blur of light and sound. "I never thought I would be anything resembling a father."

Rubi's brows furrowed. "Does that bother you?"

"No." I lacked the ability to cry, like humans did, but I felt a wave of emotion so strong, I imagined that if I could cry, I would be doing so now. "I have always longed for a connection to a child. To hold them and tell them stories. To take them on adventures and..." I trailed off, trying to grasp all the newness that had come into my life. I let out a laugh of joy and picked her up by the waist, twirling her around.

She let out a garbled whooping sound and stared wide-eyed at me when I put her back down. "Warn me when you're going to do that."

I lowered my mouth to hers. "Very well, if you will warn me when you are going to turn my life upside down."

"Hmm, can't do that," she said. "I'm just as shocked as you are. This wasn't what I expected when I came to Stryxia to visit my daughter. You weren't what I expected."

I gazed down into her dark blue eyes, which were the same as my own, now. "I thought my chance had passed. I thought my chances for love—many forms of it—had passed."

Her arms came around me and her mouth curved

into a smile that I intended to keep on her face as often as possible. Her fingers moved through my hair and her body pressed up against mine. "Surprise, Rixen. Looks like a life full of love has just begun."

Hi readers! I hope you enjoyed Rubi and Rixen's story! Please consider leaving a review. This is a story set in the (completed) Stryxian Alien Warriors series. Turn the page for a list of all my books For free stories, bonus content, and book news, sign up for my newsletter by going to my website at www.ellablakeauthor.com.

Also by Ella Blake

Craving the Heveians

VIRGO'S PRIZE

THE ALIEN'S BITE

THE ALIEN'S FIRE

THE ALIEN'S BLADE

THE ALIEN'S ESCAPE

THE ALIEN'S STEEL

THE ALIEN'S FATE

Stryxian Alien Warriors

BONDED TO THE STRYXIAN

STRANDED WITH THE STRYXIAN (free novella)

SAVED BY THE STRYXIAN

CLAIMED BY THE STRYXIAN

POSSESSED BY THE STRYXIAN

CHAINED TO THE STRYXIAN

SEDUCED BY THE STRYXIAN

The Lords of Destra

LOST TO THE ALIEN LORD

BOUND TO THE ALIEN LORD

FATED TO THE ALIEN LORD

CRAVED BY THE ALIEN LORD

DESTINED FOR THE ALIEN LORD

ENSNARED BY THE ALIEN LORD

Virilian Mail Order Mates

TRAK

DREX

VIRAK

NIIR

TARON

KIM & KLAE (novella)

SAKAR (bonus holiday book)

The Baylan Chronicles

DRACE

RAZE

ARTEN

HARC

ZADE

Made in United States
Troutdale, OR
12/04/2023